JACK RABBIT

Also by Jan Kelly

The Arizona Series
Elder Brother's Maze
Jack Rabbit
The Last Creation
Sacred Arrow
People of the Sun

Watch for more at https://ReadJanKelly.com.

Book Two of The Arizona Series:
Western / Adventure / Romance Novels
set in the Modern American West

Jan Kelly

JACK RABBIT

Book Two of the Arizona Series
Western / Adventure / Romance
Author: Jan Kelly
Copyrighted ©2018 by Jan Kelly
Published 2018 by Jan Kelly

For my father

PROLOGUE:
THE NAVAJO

Hear the stories of the People, the *Diné*. Listen:

Long ago, during the days of the ancestors, the People were hunted by the *Naayéé*, monsters who devoured all they could catch and scattered the survivors over the buttes and valleys. Changing Woman and her sister, White Shell Woman, feared for their sons' lives, but their boys were brave to the point of foolishness. They ignored their mothers' pleas to stay hidden behind their skirts and sought help in fending off these evil beings from Spider Woman.

The boys' path across the mesas was not easy, and they were dragging their feet, cold and hungry, nearly ready to turn toward home again, when they saw a wisp of smoke rising from the ground. They crept forward fearfully; there was a hole with a ladder descending into the darkness. "Anything could be down there," whispered one of the young men.

"Anything and anybody," agreed the other.

But when they poked their heads over the opening what they saw was an old woman sitting serenely before her fire. When she lifted her face to them, they saw she was smiling. And she welcomed them, saying, "Hello, my sons," in a gravelly voice. "Who are you?"

But this was not an easy question for the boys to answer, as their mothers had never divulged the names of their fathers to them. "Alas, grandmother, we only know that *his* mother is Changing Woman and mine is White Shell Woman. We've run away from them . . . ."

"We're protecting them," interrupted the other boy. "Alien monsters are eating our kinsmen, and they will eat our mothers, too, unless Spider Woman helps us to destroy them."

The old woman cackled behind one hand. "Yes," she said. "There is much I can do to help you." She gestured them down the ladder. "Come into my home in the ground. Come and tell Spider Woman all that you know."

ONE: JACK
Winslow, northern Arizona
Early June, 1994

A cloudless sky floated over the Painted Desert and the high mesa scrub lands of the Colorado Plateau, empty until a turkey vulture drifted into view. It outlined the San Francisco Mountains in a distant arc, the high point of Humphrey's Peak still trimmed with snow in early June. Then the vulture drifted south, above the bunch grass, piñons and junipers on the dry backside of the Mogollon Rim, until it was swallowed up in the dust hurtling skyward behind a racing pickup.

A column of red dust, thick as smoke, traced the truck's progress across the mesa. The sides and bed, even the roof of the cab, were badly dented, the once-blue paint marred and scraped. Its suspension was so badly shot from traveling at similar high speeds over the mud-rutted roads of the mesa top that it listed crazily toward the passenger's side and the steering wheel shuddered in Jack's hands like a vibrator bed in a cheap roadside motel room.

But Jack was paying no attention to his truck; he never did. He just drove it like hell to his next destination: the Brown Barn Saloon, Bashas' or Ray's Hay and Feed in Winslow, or the twenty miles home again to the J-Bar Ranch near Jack's Canyon on the mesa. This time he was headed home, his work-scarred hands clamped on the jittery steering wheel, his teeth clenched just as hard, his eyes squinting straight ahead, unseeing, at the horizon. He made no effort to miss the pot-holes or rocks and didn't takes his foot off the gas until he was bouncing over the cattle guard at his own fence line and skidding to a stop in the packed red dirt of his yard.

The dust settled slowly around him and the cooling engine ticked off the seconds of silence. Jack didn't take his hands off the wheel for a long time, just squeezed up his eyes, trying to shut it all out. He was scared, scared shitless, he finally admitted to himself, and his guts were hurting like hell. But none of that helped any.

Jack's old dog, Hud, had come out from under the porch at the sound of the truck on the road but had hung back, his tail in a slow wag, until he was sure the machine was off and motionless. Now he came closer to stretch and shake himself expectantly, wagging his whole back end when Jack finally turned his head to notice him out the window.

Hud was still a good range dog, interested in everything going on around the ranch, smart enough to keep out of the way of the horses and cattle. He was a Labrador-mix with a good nose for a spring or a stock pond or the infrequent pools of water in the washes, not afraid of gunfire and eager on a hunt. But he'd been a big disappointment to Jack the past few years, and the old man scowled down at him, focusing, for a time, his formless rage.

It used to be Jack and Hud were inseparable. From the time Hud was a pup—and he was almost twelve, now, with white hairs in the black fur of his muzzle—he had gone with Jack to town, riding in the cab or the bed of the truck, depending on how recently he'd been rolling in the manure pile. He'd wait outside the restaurant or store, bored but undistractable, no matter who or what went by, until Jack finally finished up his business and strolled out the door.

Then the moment Hud set eyes on Jack, he would be beside himself with joy. He'd bound around him in circles, whipping his thick Lab tail. People would stop on the street to watch, and if they stood too close, they got their knees walloped—Jack had seen that tail knock the feet out from under a ten-year-old. Jack always made like it was no big deal to him, cursed the dog back into the truck, then left a streak of rubber on the pavement as he peeled out onto the street.

But several years ago they'd been out in the truck together, driving along one of the dirt roads dissecting the ranch, checking on the new fence they'd strung to keep the cattle out of a section of range scheduled for a rest. The Blue Grama grass was thick and enticing on the rotated section, and Jack had plenty of sympathy for the yearling steer trying to push his way back to his old range, his head stuck through the low wires of the fence.

On the other hand, Jack was also particular about his fences, just as his dad had been before him. Jack Senior had marked off the boundaries of his property with wooden posts sunk a foot deep in the rocky soil, strung tight with double-barbed wire. Jack had added miles of new fences, this time to outline grazing areas rather than property boundaries, and had employed two men to "ride fence" year-round once he took over the operation. Over the years, section by section, they'd replaced the wood with spaded steel posts, strung new wire, and put in cattle guards at every road crossing. And now this homesick steer was putting it all to the test.

Jack had swerved off the road and jounced over the scrub sage and grass of the mesa, the steering wheel spinning out of his hands as he careened through the brush. This was nothing new to Jack—he'd been tearing through this landscape since he was old enough to reach the pedals of his dad's old flatbed—and the gully he hit at too high a speed was nothing new to Jack, either. He'd wrecked enough trucks to keep Clark's Auto in business, or so he'd bragged more than once down at the Brown Barn.

This time the slip-rock lip of the gully sent his right front-end flying at the same time the driver's side wheel hit sand. His speed and angle were great enough to flip the truck neatly on its back, the engine still racing and the tires spinning in the face of a blank blue sky.

Jack had landed in a corner of the roof, all bunched up around his shoulder. He found the key in the ignition, turned it the wrong way, grinding the starter, then got it right and shut the engine off. It was a tight squeeze out the window, but as soon as he'd gotten his breath back, Jack crawled out and hobbled over to kick the damn steer away from the fence.

He heard Hud's whimper but ignored him and finished checking the wire; he'd been cited for grazing violations too often in the past.

Every year the U.S. Forest Service sent a college kid around with a clipboard, and allowing cattle into the rested area would mean a big black check mark on the form and a fine high enough to boil Jack's blood. And if it wasn't the Forest Service kid it was the BLM's "range specialist," or the state's Game and Fish guy—Jack was certain that if a steer's nose crossed the line there'd be somebody with a clipboard there to note it.

Only when Jack was satisfied with the condition of his fence did he take a good look at what he'd done to the truck. The cab had landed inside the wash but the bed rested flat on the higher ground. Hud had been riding in the back and was now attempting to dig his way out, his black claws scratching frantically at the sandstone. When his nose appeared, Jack hollered at him to "stay" and started the long walk back to the ranch.

About halfway there he met up with one of the hands he'd hired on for the May roundup—out on a joy ride, Jack decided, since all the vaccinating, branding, ear-marking and castrating that day was going on at the farthest of the ranch's three main corrals. Jack commandeered the man's horse without explanation. Then when he got to the machine shed, he started up the tractor they used for winter feed runs and began the slow return ride to the truck. Hud was hoarse from barking by the time Jack had hooked the chain to the rear axle and started winching the truck back onto its tires.

The tools, rags, oil cans and hay were still scattered on the ground, but the dog took off as soon as he saw daylight, not even looking around at Jack. When Hud had made it back to the ranch house he'd holed up under the porch and stayed there through most of the next day, coming out only for the water Jack's daughter, Kate, set out by the tunnel the dog had clawed deep into the shade under the house.

Ever since then, whenever Jack went near his truck, Hud disappeared, and no amount of coaxing or cursing could get him out from under that porch. Jack berated the dog as a coward to anyone who'd listen after that. He even thought about getting another dog, but he never did. It was a lonely drive to town, now, and nobody gave a shit when he decided to climb back in the repaired truck to head home. But the worst part was Jack knew the damn dog had lost faith in him. And that hurt.

Hud sat down, then laid down, when Jack made no move to emerge from the truck. The dog would look over, panting and grinning, from time to time but keeping his distance, as always, from the machine. And Jack glowered back at the dog. He was certainly no comfort to him, Jack decided—not anymore; the mutt was really starting to show his age. Even from this distance Jack could make out the whitened whiskers, the gauntness at the hips where the puppy had been like a coiled spring. There was not much time left for either of them.

That thought finally pushed Jack from the truck and across the yard, with Hud following at his heels. Jack avoided the wood-frame, two-story house his father had built and headed for the trailer beside it that had been his home for the past two years. It was cramped and sparsely furnished—really only intended for use during their fall roundup, when they moved cattle off the forest land on the Mogollon Plateau to over-winter at the ranch—but it suited Jack much better than sharing the house with his daughter and his new son-in-law.

He threw his weight against the door to push it open but then stopped there on the steps. Hud had already settled down in his spot on the shady side of the trailer and dropped his head onto his paws. But Jack looked into the musty little kitchen and decided not to go in. Even with all the windows and the door open it was stifling hot at this time of the day; the lumpy spot on the broken-down couch where he usually sat looked as defeated and vacant as he felt inside.

Behind him the land—his land—spread out on three sides to the horizon, more than 16,000 acres, counting the leased holdings in the Coconino Forest that bordered his property on the south and west. This had been his place for sixty-eight years; he'd learned ranching, riding and roping from the original cowboys who'd homesteaded this open country along with his father and his grandfather before him. And he'd be damned if he was going to leave it all now. It was impossible, unacceptable. He left the trailer door hanging ajar and Hud scrambled up to follow him to the house.

Jack heard activity in the barn as he walked past—probably Fred, shoveling out a stall or messing with one of the horses. But Jack didn't stop to give orders and criticize as he normally would have. He'd always prided himself on the fact that he had never punched a clock for a living, had portioned out every day of his life to match the progress of the sun. Now he felt an unfamiliar urgency, a steady ticking in the bottom of his gut.

Both cars were gone from the drive alongside the house; his son-in-law would still be at the Winslow high school, but Jack had no idea where his daughter was off to. He was just glad she was out somewhere for a change, instead of haunting the house, meddling in his business, as usual.

Jack slipped through the screen door quietly, closing it in Hud's face. His daughter had been spoiling the mutt, letting him snooze on the cool tiles under the table, feeding him scraps, things Jack had never allowed. Jack crept up the stairs, and the insidious ticking of the old clock on the downstairs mantel made more noise than he did as he moved down the carpeted hallway. He held even his breath when he stopped in his bedroom doorway.

Only now it was his daughter's room, Jack's one concession to her marriage to Richard two years ago. He'd told Katie the bigger room with the four-poster double bed was his wedding present to the two of them, and the girl had gone soft-eyed and thrown her arms around his neck, embarrassing him.

But giving up his room hadn't really reconciled him to their new arrangement. Right away, Katie had taken over more than just the bed Jack had shared with his own wife; she'd pulled down from the attic his wife's favorite landscape painting and the woven bedspread she'd ordered out of the catalogue, moved the lady's mirrored dressing table back into the corner by the window, and placed the old porcelain pitcher and wash basin in the center of its doilied dresser-top. Even Katie's mannerisms, lately, were eerily reminiscent of the woman Jack had himself married.

Of course it was nothing new for Jack to be troubled by his daughter. She'd been the first child born to him and Lucy, and even as a pink and squalling infant she had started the icy silence between them, since Lucy had known how much Jack had wanted a son. But that was all right when Lucy conceived again, until the big boy-child she produced after a nearly ten month pregnancy and hours of struggle on this very bed was presented to him wrapped in a blanket like an over-sized doll, blue-lipped and cold. John Stegner Rawlings IV died seconds later, still cradled in Jack's arms, while his wife moaned and tossed with a fever and women huddled nervously around her.

Nothing had been the same after that, not Lucy, who seldom left her bed until pneumonia finally took her that winter, not his daughter, Katie, who cried incessantly for what seemed like the next two years, and never his own dreams for the future.

Jack pushed himself the rest of the way into the bedroom and sat down, suddenly very weary, on the edge of the bed. If he let himself lie back, he knew he'd be dozing in an instant. But Jack still believed naps were a waste of time that only babies could indulge in without shame. He'd have to be a damn sight older and sicker before he'd succumb to such laziness himself. On the other hand, he spent most afternoons nowadays in a kind of dazed review of the past, sometimes blurring whatever he was up to with whatever he had used to do so well.

Jack sat ruminating with his hands on his knees, then grunted as he leaned over and yanked open the bottom drawer of his daughter's dresser. He remembered now what he was looking for—a small, ornate box containing a few brooches and earrings that had belonged to his wife and a single key—and he found it under a pile of shawls and scarves without difficulty. His daughter had had the same hiding place since she was a child.

Jack pocketed the key, snapped the box shut, and replaced it. Then he dug around some more to find the other box he knew was in there, pulled it out and sifted through the photographs on top. That whole layer was Katie's—pictures of her wedding and recent shots of her husband's family in Flagstaff—but underneath was an old framed picture of his wife, Lucy, her lips and eyes tinted with color, her hair a sepia brown. Jack held it up and squinted at it, then laid it beside him on the bedspread and sorted through the even older photographs, keepsakes and documents to find the bottom of the box.

His grandfather, the first Jack, had grown up on the gulf coast of Texas and fought the Mexicans alongside his own father to carve a ranch out of a palmetto-studded wilderness. There was nothing that old in Katie's box, and Jack had never met the man, but the stories he'd heard as a boy had fired a steely-eyed hero in his imagination, so Jack could imagine him, plain as day, a young, square-jawed man journeying out here to the Arizona territory with his new wife, Grace, and a small herd of longhorns. Jack's Canyon was first recorded on a railroad surveyor's 1880 map, and later that same year, Grace had fed the railroad construction crew its Christmas dinner at her own board-and-saw-horse table.

Katie did have Jack dad's spurs, double mounted silver with cracked leather straps. Jack Senior had been born right here on the J-Bar ranch, in 1886, during a decade-long drought. But Grandpa Jack had homesteaded along perennial water—Jack's Canyon was dissected by a little stream that, over the eons, had carved deep channels through the limestone. And both the family and the ranch had not just survived but grown during those ten years of drought, as Grandpa Jack kept on acquiring land, 160-acres at a time, buying up every seep or catchment basin he could find.

A brittle yellow newspaper article showed Jack's dad and his uncles lined up on their mounts for a rodeo parade. That whole generation had grown up on horseback. They'd heard first-hand the account of Geronimo's defeat and celebrated statehood by emptying their pistols at the clouds, their bellies sloshing whiskey. Jack barked out a laugh. He'd come from good stock; the five men rode tall in the saddle, square shouldered, wearing their town hats and Sunday shirts. They'd weathered good and bad times, though mostly bad, and had even managed to keep the ranch alive despite Roosevelt's new-fangled conservation measures, more drought and the Great Depression.

Jack's discharge papers were in the unsealed envelope he set aside. He'd had the misfortune of being in the service during the best years the ranch had seen—they'd stocked more cattle during WWII than they ever had, before or since. He'd come home from the war sick to death of foreign places and with one, single-minded goal: he would carry on the J-Bar, only now it would be his—his own family's—lasting empire. Then Jack had lost his wife, had lost his son and heir, and now the one offspring he had managed to produce was caving in to the feds, the clowns with the clipboards, and was close to losing just about everything his father and grandfather had worked so hard for so many years to pass on to him.

Jack let his chin drop to his chest and heaved a great sigh. His hands, fat-knuckled with arthritis and healed-over bones, scarred by all the nicks and burns and other insults he'd submitted them to over the years, settled heavily on the contents of the box on his lap. Those early losses had nearly defeated him. He'd married late, and when Lucy had died he was already thirty-eight. He hadn't been able to imagine going through all the trouble of courting a woman again. Besides, he had already bought out his uncles' interest in the ranch and now had all the work he could handle, not to mention a whining little girl who clung to his leg until he had to pry her loose, and who hid behind the furniture like a frightened rabbit whenever anyone except the old woman he'd hired to care for her came into the house.

Another newspaper clipping showed a younger version of himself, all barbered up, announcing he'd been elected to the school board a few years back. Jack dropped that back in the pile with a grin. His tenure had been short and explosive, but only because Jack wouldn't deign to engage in any of their politicking. He'd just spoken his mind when and how he wanted to with no regard for anybody's "rules." It had confirmed his and all of Winslow's suspicion that he just wasn't "town fit."

But did he mind? Hell, no. So what if all he'd ever been good at was working cattle, because there could be no doubt in any sane person's mind that Jack had been one hell of a wrangler. And wasn't it really the ranch that had saved him? He'd spent more days on horseback the year his wife had died than he cared to remember, even now; more hours staring at steers' backsides than he could ever forget. Sometimes he still wondered if he had really been inspecting the herd for pink eye and hoof rot, scouting strays and checking water tanks, or just riding in circles to keep alive. He'd spend a week crossing the ranch with two pack horses loaded down with posts, wire, fence stretchers, pliers, a hammer and a shovel, then after a couple of hot showers and five or six meals eaten in his own kitchen, he'd be ready to saddle up and trace the circuit again.

That's how the ranch had grown under him; his hard work had paid off. Jack hadn't acquired any new privately-owned acreage, but he'd bullied and cajoled the BLM and the Forest Service into larger allotments than any of his forebears had overseen. Jack had owned the water rights—that was the key. The only way the feds had been able to make any money off those parcels was by leasing them to him. They'd tried to make him follow way too many rules, that was true, some that Jack could barely stomach—what the hell made a stream a riparian area, anyway? And weren't cows just as much a part of nature as a god-damned fish? But Jack had followed the rest-rotation system closely enough to build the herd back up to the 372 head he was authorized to graze from spring through the fall. And, by God, despite what his daughter said, he wasn't through with this business yet.

Jack picked up the photo of his wife again and fingered the silver frame nervously. He'd done this before—he'd sneaked up here to look at the stuff he'd ordered his daughter to remove from the table downstairs, after yelling at her for cluttering up his house with sentimental junk and threatening to toss the whole lot in the trash if he ever laid eyes on any of it again. The other times it had made him feel better, superior somehow. After all, he'd survived, and all the other people in these dog-eared photographs—his mom and dad standing on the porch when the house was brand new, Lucy smiling before the stove they'd bought just after they were married, the old daguerreotypes of a fat German great aunt, a skinny Irish one—were all dead and gone. Even the big old Texas longhorn bull Jack had kept in that front pasture for years—his daughter, Katie, was in this picture, halfway up the fence, still in pigtails—was nothing but brittle bones and dust by now.

But this time his wife's face seemed disconcertingly familiar. She'd slept right beside him on this bed, after all, waking even before him to cook breakfast for anywhere up to fifteen men. And most nights she'd crawled back in under the covers long after he'd collapsed; Jack remembered hearing her still banging around in the kitchen while he stretched out, his hands folded on his chest. Jack felt badly about how seldom he'd stopped to think of her like this. It had seemed so important at the time to go on living, to fill up the spaces she'd occupied in his heart, that he'd kind of stopped believing in her. Now, today, she was real again.

"Daddy?"

Jack dropped the picture into the box and looked up, scowling. How long had the girl been standing there in the doorway, spying on him? "What?" he growled.

Katie sighed and brushed a hand down the front of her dress. Jack had lost track of how many months pregnant she was, but he noticed now that her belly was big enough to precede her into the room. She didn't answer his question, just looked pointedly at the box in his hands, then back at her father. "What did the doctor say?" she asked.

Katie was a pretty girl, but the forlorn look in her eyes turned her appearance into something different, something childlike and desperate. Even her long dark hair—the same dark waves her mother had worn back in a braid—looked hang-dog and bedraggled to Jack.

He just snorted and stood up. He hated this—being caught with his pants down, so to speak. He thought about stuffing the box back in the drawer and then just dropped it on the bed behind him and pushed past his daughter, gripping the railing with one hand, cradling his sore gut with the other, trying not to hurry too obviously down the stairs.

"Dad. He got the tests back, right?" She stayed at the head of the steps—at least she wasn't following him. "I thought you went in to get the results today."

"I did," he said, waving her off. Jack let the screen door slap behind him, then fingering the stolen key in his pocket, he allowed the rage to boil out of him. "One hundred and fifty god-damned dollars for the son-of-a-bitch to sit at his fancy desk and make his holy pronouncement. Well, he can wait for his money 'till hell freezes over, him and the god-damned bankers and the god-damned, lousy government. I'm not done yet, you hear me? So all a' ya can just quit peckin' at me like a bunch of damned vultures."

The dog trailed him across the yard, but when Jack yanked open the door of his truck, Hud turned around, trotted back to the house, and crept in under the porch.

TWO: RABBIT

They say everyone has a story, and if you think about it, it's true—we all have *several* stories, in fact. There's the love stories that produced us and the ones we created ourselves. There's our birth stories and the tales of our adventures. And eventually, there are the stories that others will tell about us, the ones that end with how we died.

* * * * *

My father was the kind of man who invariably sent my visiting girlfriends home in tears. Some never got past the scowl he'd have on his face as he answered the door, others lasted long enough to help me pull the Barbies out of the closet, but they'd wither quickly under the scorn he would heap on us for playing with such worthless toys. Why did he follow us up to my room, I wonder even now. This man took no interest in my schooling, never signed me up for summer camps or swimming lessons, could care less if I had clean clothes to wear or brushed my teeth or ate anything other than peanut butter scraped from the jar onto a cracker. He was too busy for me—he'd be already in the yard barking orders when I crawled out of bed each morning and was usually still outside when I curled with a book under the covers again. So on these special occasions—and they were so rare they really qualified as "special"—why did he hover outside the door? Was he worried about what I would do or say to these little girls? Or did he come running when he heard the plastic whisper of the Barbie Dressing Box as I pulled it down from the shelf?

I have to admit, though—he's right. I mean, it was true then and still is that neither I nor even the best endowed of my childhood friends would ever match Barbie's measurements. Still, it is cruel to point out these things to nine-year-olds still nursing hopes of an ideal future.

If they took my father's remarks as teasing—and some did—they could stick it out for the real event, as the criticism gradually turned from our toys to general complaints about "kids these days" to the specific: me or, sadly, the hapless child I had bribed into visiting. Even the promise of a necklace or pin, or the chance to see a two-headed calf (which never existed—I made that one up) could never compensate for the ridicule we endured of our hairstyles (women in Dad's day would never cut their hair this short), our freckled skin (my mother, Dad would inform us—had died with a complexion still as white and clear as bone china), or our manners (we were too loud, we were brazen, we talked back).

Once the standard attack was completed, Dad would zero in with incredible accuracy on the one failing or insecurity we suffered most over in private—buck teeth, hairy arms, adolescent clumsiness—and he'd drag it out like a trampled rug that needed a thorough whacking. Why is he so good at this, I often wondered, watching numbly as he pressed his attack. He never gave me that much attention when I was alone.

The softer girls would sob before and after the phone calls to their mothers, begging for a ride home. I admired the ones who stormed out the door, refusing to give my father the satisfaction of their tears, even if it meant a nearly impossible 20 mile hike back to town. Dad would wait while I put away whatever toys I'd pulled out—in tears myself, but not angry, really, since it had become so inevitable—then I would ride in the bed of the truck while he bounced us down the dirt lane toward the road. And even the most stalwart girl would have lost much of her steam by then, having made it to the blacktop where she could see how the ribbon of the highway narrowed to a thin line at the horizon. These friendships were over by the time the girl climbed over the tailgate and crouched beside me, but I still enjoyed the company, sitting with our backs against the cab of the truck, the wind whipping our hair and sending specks of straw into our eyes. For those few minutes, we had to hang on tight and get through this together. When Dad finally slammed on the brakes before the other child's house I'd think: There—now she knows why I'm like this.

But I didn't really understand my father or myself until we read Faulkner's "A Rose for Emily" during my junior year of high school. Books had long replaced those thwarted grade school friendships; the stories were immutable—Dad could tear into them as much as he wanted without even slowing the progress of my eyes down the page. I would read whole shelves of the school library's collections. If I found an author I liked, I'd read everything he or she had ever published. I would read compulsively every book that made up a series, from Doctor Doolittle to Nancy Drew to the *Alexandrian Quartet*. But I'd never seen myself on a page before Faulkner put me there.

The tableau in "A Rose for Emily" shocks me—it's like looking in a mirror. The only difference is that my father, framed by that open door, would have been holding a shotgun instead of a horsewhip. Then I realized that the whole story was about me, that it predicted my spinsterhood, my descent into insanity. We, my father and I, formed the western version of that old Southern Order, the last of a family so possessive of its blood and land that no outsider could ever be worthy of helping us continue them.

And it would have happened—those gray hairs on the pillow would have been mine—if I hadn't met Richard.

THREE: ROSE

I run. That's who I am, it's what I do, it's what I've always done. I think I was about 5 the first time I took off. Lily was trying to dump me again at some nursery school. We'd been there a few times, peanut butter sandwiches served at tiny tables, and I'd eyed the trash cans out front on, like, our second time, and fantasized about jumping into one and hiding there until she'd driven off, but instead I made an outright dash for it. She snagged me before I cleared the driveway, hauled me screaming into the office. I remember the pre-school lady didn't want to take my arm but Lily insisted, and I was squirming and flailing around, but then as soon as the bitch left I stopped the act. What the hell. I liked peanut butter. I still do.

This suicide, it's really no different. It's a leap into the inevitable unknown. I honestly don't know why anyone prefers to just sit around and wait for death when you can conjure it up any time you want to. Or almost any time, depending on how you're gonna die, of course. That's kind of what's stopping me. I'm a little short on resources these days.

But it's not that I'm depressed. Yes, I do take a bunch of pills for that kind of crap. They make us at the group home. And I took them when Lily used to give them to me. They can all go ahead and dope me as much as they want—I'm still determined to get the hell out of here. It's just an instinct with me. Some people get mad when they're faced with all this crap that's so unfair and stupid. I used to—I got to be an expert at throwing fits, screaming and shit. It makes people crazy—crazier than me. And sometimes I used to want to take a stand and fight, even though I always knew it was a f-ing waste of time and I was never going to win, anyway, so I'd scream and bite and claw like some f-ing animal until they tied me up.

Some people cower. I'm kinda doing that every time I just close this journal, shut off my flashlight, throw off the blanket, roll over and shut my eyes. But what I want to do, what I really wish I could do, is run. I want to take that leap, I do. I think I really do.

FOUR

First one boy and then the other stepped cautiously onto the ladder. The boy on the lowest rung said, "Our mothers never married."

The boy above him said, "For all we know, our fathers are the tall and round cactus." He snickered but fell silent when the other boy glared up at him.

"I will tell you who your fathers are," the old woman said. "Come on," she coaxed them, "enter my home."

So the boys dropped one by one into her chamber and sat with the old woman around her fire. "The waterfall sired you," she told White Shell Woman's son. "Your mother was lonely with only her sister for company. She felt herself changing from a girl into a woman and sought comfort in the mountain stream." Then Spider Woman turned her attention to Changing Woman's child. "Your mother sensed the spirit life inside the sun. Every day for four days she lay on a rock and watched its travels from one horizon to the next. You are the result of that warmth she was basking in. It's *your* father, young man, whose help you two should seek."

The boys exchanged a look. Mountain Stream and Sun were much better fathers than the tall and round cacti they'd imagined. Each sat up taller. They smacked their lips as they ate the food the old woman prepared for them and smiled at one another over her fire.

"Why are you two grinning like that?" Spider Woman scolded them when she looked up from stirring the pot. "Your journey to your father's house will be filled with peril—rocks will try to crush you, reeds will seek to slash you, cacti will tear you to shreds if they can, and then you'll still have to cross the sands that turn all travelers to ash."

The boys' chewing slowed and their eyes grew so wide with fear that the old woman couldn't help but laugh. "Okay, don't worry so much. I said I would help you." Spider Woman settled herself again in her seat by the fire. "I'll give you a charm—a charm and a magic song, okay? You'll have the power you need to help yourselves and your people. You must remember: it is always possible, even in the midst of great danger, to walk in beauty."

FIVE

The reddish light of early morning fell through the open window of the trailer's bathroom and onto the warped vinyl flooring at Jack's feet. He squeezed his eyes shut, straining to eliminate the blood-slick poison from his bowels, and cursed the doctor with each quick breath. Then he cradled his head, weak and remorseful, and waited for the strength to wipe himself, pull up his pants, and stumble back to his bed.

He had spent all yesterday afternoon at the Brown Barn, sitting off in a corner at a table by himself, for a change, brooding and knocking back Budweisers. On the way home, he'd eaten that greasy burger at the Sonic, his battered old pick-up surrounded by teenagers in their daddies' cars. And it had gotten pretty late because that ditzy little curb-hopper had made him sit there—fuming—while she socialized with her pals through windows rolled up just enough to take the clamps of the tray.

He'd been so low and sorrowful going home through the dark landscape that he'd pretended Hud was there on the seat beside him with his chin thrust into the wind, ears flapping. Jack had pounded on the steering wheel and threatened out loud that, if he couldn't lick this thing, he was damn sure going to take someone with him. Maybe that no-account doctor. Maybe someone else.

Now, staggering back to bed, Jack thought maybe it was all bluster. Maybe he was already too sick to do anybody any damage. He cocked his head to look out the window at the house, suddenly missing his dead wife with an unfamiliar acuteness, and turned around to shuffle out the trailer's flimsy door toward it in his bedroom slippers, shirtless, holding his pants up with one hand and balancing himself with the other.

Hud met him at the door and whined a greeting through the screen. "You rotten traitor son-of-a-bitch," Jack sputtered, feigning outrage. "You've gone soft as butter in your old age—sleeping in the house! Worthless piece of shit." But Hud kept wagging his tail happily—Jack's tirade had been delivered in a toneless whisper—and followed his master's halting steps through the hall and into the kitchen.

Katie's husband, Richard—or Mr. Crawford, as Jack sometimes still thought of him, since that was how he'd been introduced during Jack's brief term on the school board—was at the long table eating a bowl of cereal, an open book in front of him. He towered over Jack when he was standing, but hunched over his cereal Richard looked like your typical, narrow-chested school teacher, right down to the thick, black-rimmed glasses perched on his nose.

Jack leaned against the counter, torn between the reluctance that always overcame him at the sight of his son-in-law and the need to sit before he fell.

"Hey, Jack," Richard said, finally looking up from the page. "You okay? You don't look so good."

"Same to you," Jack muttered. But his legs were winning the battle, so he pulled out a chair and dropped into it with a heart-felt groan.

"Here, have something to eat. Maybe that'll help." Richard set the box of Cheerios down in front of him. "Want me to get you a bowl?" he asked, rising—eager to please as always. But Jack just glared at him, and Richard sat back down. "How about a glass of milk, at least? You've got to keep up your strength." Jack dropped his stony gaze to the table in front of him, shaking his head. "We missed you at dinner last night," Richard added, winding down.

"I ate," Jack informed him. "Where is she?"

"Kate?" Richard asked, a spoonful of cereal half-way to his mouth. "She's still sleeping. Or trying to—I guess these last few weeks are pretty hard on a woman." Richard smiled at Jack while finishing his breakfast, as proud of his wife's pregnancy, Jack was thinking, as if he'd invented the whole damn process himself.

Jack found himself feeling better, sitting across from his son-in-law and musing about what a fool Richard was—book-learnin' only goes so far in this world, he was fond of saying. Maybe that's why he had lasted just half a term on the school board, that kind of thinking and the little arguments he was prone to, though he'd restrained himself and had thrown only one punch at the high school principal, who was a much younger man and plenty able to defend himself.

And since he was feeling more like his old self, Jack's thoughts turned again to his increasingly elaborate plan: how he could hole up somewhere—probably the attic, with its barricade-able trap door and two small windows—to make his stand. He didn't need no hospital, no matter how sick he got. And if the bastards tried to take him from his home, he'd shoot them all, one by one, and die like his grandfather had, a stand-up man protecting himself and his property.

Jack relished the account of his Grandpa Jack's valiant death, although his father certainly hadn't. Jack Senior would never discuss the incident. He'd been only twelve at the time, the oldest of five boys, and the loss—and the shock of sudden manhood—had been hard on him. But Jack had heard the story many times from the cowboys inhabiting the bunkhouse through the years. Although none of the original witnesses remained by the time Jack was old enough to work with the outfit, others had picked up the tale; it was passed with the whiskey bottle around the campfire. And every cowboy had his own two bits to add.

Jack never questioned any of the details, even in the conflicting accounts, and he never tired of hearing the story. He would sit up straight and bask in the reflected glory of his legendary progenitor every time a wrangler pushed back his hat and started the account: "Mr. Rawlings, he's a damn fine cowman, but his daddy was the real original. Now *he* was a man, my friends, who knew cattle. He could tell with a glance at a herd if there was any strays—and who they belonged to. He could point out an animal and tell ya how that heifer or bull or steer was the calf of such and such a cow. Why, he could ride anything with hair on it, and he was a damn fine roper, too."

How could such a young man—Grandpa Jack had only been in his thirties—have felt so strongly, have been willing to give up so much, his very life, over a bull? Maybe it had been a proven sire, the only surviving long horn bull from the herd he'd brought out with him from Texas, or maybe he'd finally just had enough of the Hashknife rustlers—Jack had heard it both ways.

"You sure you don't want some breakfast, Jack?" Richard was clearing the table, water rushing into the sink behind him. Jack realized he was starting to wash the dishes.

"Don't you got some work you got to go to?" Jack asked.

"Not this week." Richard came over to wipe the table with a dishcloth, and Jack had to lift his elbows out of the way. "Summer school doesn't start until the 20th. I could make you some toast, if you'd like."

Next thing he'll be offering to fry me an egg, Jack thought, smirking and rubbing the stubble on his chin. "Naw, you go ahead with what you're doing there," he said. "I got something to attend to in the office." He hoisted himself carefully from the chair.

"You know Kate doesn't like you messing around in there," Richard reminded him over his shoulder, his hands in the sudsy water.

But Jack just grunted at him as he made his way to the little pantry off the kitchen that Katie called her office. "Won't take but a minute," Jack assured him, and he shut the door in Hud's face before the dog could follow him in.

The storeroom was cool and dimly lit; Jack alternated between rubbing his chest and arms for warmth and tugging up his pants as he waited for his eyes to adjust. Canned goods and sacks of potatoes and onions lined one wall, but Katie had moved a desk in under the little window and Jack felt his way over to it and sat down.

Normally she'd catch him in here thumbing through one of the ledgers; it had annoyed Jack no end when she'd taken over his books and started paying his bills. Jack had had his own method of bookkeeping for years, but one little IRS audit had changed all that. Jack had been given two choices by his banker in town: hire an accountant to keep accurate records or turn the books over to his daughter. Jack had picked the lesser of two evils.

For awhile he'd still kept his hand in, standing over Katie's shoulder after supper as she labored to decipher his checks, made stacks of feed and veterinary bills, marked old invoices "paid" or "outstanding," and worried over the payroll taxes. Jack would bluster and complain and down half a bottle of whiskey before she'd slam the book shut and stomp off to her room. The next day he'd catch her on the way to or back from town with a grocery sack full of forms and ledgers; Jack couldn't guess at the time who was helping her. Now he figured it had been Richard, and it made him think it must have been a sorry courtship, indeed.

Jack had been carrying the little key in his pants' pocket since he'd swiped it from Katie's room. He leaned over in the chair, dug it out, fitted it into the lock in the bottom desk drawer, and jiggled it around until it turned in his fingers.

The gun box was right in front and inside was the pearl-handled .25 he'd bought the girl for her sixteenth birthday. Jack pulled it out and weighed it in his hand. It was small enough to conceal—unlike the shotguns and rifles in his gun rack, which he couldn't get to anyway, since Katie had run a bicycle lock through the handles of the case. And just as deadly at close range.

Jack opened the chamber and found it empty. He rummaged through the contents of the box, found oil, a rod and rags but no bullets, then yanked open the middle desk drawer and felt around among the pencils, pens and paper clips. Just like a god-damned woman, Jack fumed. Now how the hell was she supposed to protect herself with an unloaded gun? Make that an unloaded gun in a locked drawer with the key all the way in a whole other room of the house.

Of course Jack knew the answer to that, knew that she never planned to use it, that she'd always hated this gun, though she'd pretended to be pleased with the gift and had stoically endured his lessons that same summer. She would screw up her whole face to aim, then flinch at each report, chewing up the fence posts and the dirt for several yards around the targets, until Jack relented and let her watch him pop the cans off, one by one. Since then she'd tucked the pistol away in one hiding place or another. It had always been Jack's job to protect her and the rest of his property—and it still was.

The sound of Katie's voice in the kitchen got Jack moving again. He closed and locked the drawer, stood up and did a slow pirouette in the middle of the floor. Either the handle or the barrel stuck out of his pocket. He needed a shirt to hide the pistol if he stuck it in the waistband of his trousers; besides, it'd probably fall through, the way his pants fit him these days. He could hear her whining at Richard for letting him in the office, so Jack leaned over the desk and struggled to open the window. He heard the pistol drop with a thud into the flower bed just as Katie opened the door.

"Dad, come on," she fussed from the doorway, "you know I'll show you anything you want if you'll just ask me."

Jack waved her to silence. "It's about time you crawled out of the sack," he grumbled as he tried to squeeze past her, but it wouldn't work; she had to step back into the kitchen. "How about some god-damned breakfast? I'm like to starve around here."

* * * * *

Katie made him oatmeal and dry toast, which Jack ate noisily while he squinted at the livestock price index in the newspaper. Beef was still down, and he ranted about that until Richard excused himself and took his book out onto the porch with him. Katie, of course, was harder to get rid of.

"Are you ever going to tell me what Dr. Levy said?" she asked, sitting across the table from him, her hands clasped on the tablecloth and her doleful eyes resting on him heavily. "Do I have to call him and find out for myself?"

"Some people," Jack said, addressing Hud, as he often did when he wanted to evade answering his daughter, "don't know how to mind their own bidness. Dogs got it better than people, in that regard." Hud was curled up on the floor between them; he raised his eyebrows at Jack's words, then looked at Katie and back to Jack without moving his head from his paws.

"Dad, why do you want me to worry? If the tests say you're fine, then you're fine, right? If not, well . . . ." Katie reached over and touched one of Jack's gnarled hands. "Daddy, I want to help."

Jack pushed himself away from the table and used the back of the chair to hoist himself up. "Hell, girl, when's the last time your old man asked for anybody's help, huh? You look to your own concerns." He yanked at his pants and pointed with his chin out the kitchen window. "I guess I better get to ranching. Looks like that husband of yours has found his perch for the day." Richard had pulled the rocker over to the shady side of the porch and was framed by the open curtains, reading, pulling at his sideburns in deep concentration.

"There's nothing for you to do out there, Dad." Katie had dropped her face into her hands, and her words came out muffled. But she raised her head to go on, one cheek resting on her palm. "Chuck's still got Tom and Jimmy with him on the Rim. They've moved the herd over to the Leonard Point section."

"What? We still got cattle left?" Jack interrupted. He knew Katie had been selling stock, even at these miserable prices.

But she didn't even pause to listen. "There's still water in the Aztec stock tank, but they were worried it was too low for the calves. I guess they were trying to rig something."

"Damn it, that Chuck ain't got a brain in his head. I told him that section weren't fit for calves," Jack sputtered. "It don't take no genius to figure. Most years we never hit that point until fall, for God's sake."

"Dad, you know it's not Chuck's call. We're following the Forest Service schedule."

"Damn it, girl." Jack leaned down to slam the table with his fist. "Last year, right after the May round-up, we went just as far as Turkey Seep. I know that for a fact, 'cause I was right there on Maggie. . . ."

"You were there, Dad," Katie said, interrupting him, "making Chuck miserable—I remember that. But you weren't on Maggie. You haven't ridden in years."

It surprised Jack that his daughter would say such a thing to him, and he paused long enough that Kate kept talking. "It doesn't matter, anyway," she said, rising with one hand on her belly. "The schedule is different every year." She sighed and glanced at him as she cleared his dishes off the table. "Dad, I know it confuses you. It's gotten very complicated."

"Well, to hell with you. You sound just like them damn bureaucrats—tear up a man's land into so many puzzle pieces and just see if he can figure out how to fit 'em together enough to feed his damn family, not to mention a measly 300 head of cattle." Jack's stomach was souring all over again, and he had to stop and swallow back his breakfast.

"Two hundred and eighty," she corrected him. "Anyway, I'm sorry, Dad, but that's just the way things are." Kate was gazing out the window over the sink. When she turned to face him, Jack noticed for the first time the dark circles under her eyes.

"God damn it all to hell," Jack muttered, giving up. "It's the damn conservationists done all this. That husband of yours, for instance," he was shuffling toward the door now, keeping his voice down, "would rather feed our grass to those eight foot rabbits than put meat on his own table." Jack had loved hunting since he was a boy—had bagged his own share of elk, too—but now "wildlife" had become a dirty word to him. He made a mental note to take out as many of the critters as he could fix in his rifle sites—add that to the plan, he decided.

Richard looked up momentarily when Jack pushed his way out onto the porch, and for a moment Jack was tempted to shift the attack to his son-in-law. The no-account school teacher had had the nerve to subscribe to the Sierra Club magazine and have it mailed right here, to Jack's own home address, an outrage Jack never let rest for long. But then he remembered he had some unfinished business outside the storeroom window to attend to.

The pistol had landed butt-first in the soft dirt of the flower bed and planted itself there like a strange silver flower. Jack was glad to see no dirt had gotten into the barrel; he brushed off the pearl handle and hurried in his gimpy, bow-legged way over to his trailer where he hid the pistol under a cushion of the broken-down couch.

Then he dug out the pills he'd squirreled away in an empty cereal box in the cupboard and laid them out on the counter—those damn doctors knew what they were up to, Jack thought bitterly. If the disease didn't kill you, you'd choke to death on all the pills they gave you. But if he did manage to get them down he usually felt better, so Jack stood at the sink and swallowed them, little pink ones, a big yellow tablet, and two blue capsules, one by one, washing the mess down with gulps of warm water from the gallon jug on the counter.

As he pulled a shirt off the hanger in the tiny closet he thought about "the plan" again. The fort idea appealed to him the most, but that would pretty much take care of itself when the time came. Right now he needed to concentrate on revenge, and to do that he needed a focus for this shapeless anger that was eating him up inside. And the more he thought about it, the more sure he was that Doc Levy wouldn't do—that old wimpy fool was no good as an enemy, to Jack's way of thinking. He needed someone else, someone—or thing—worthy of his wrath. But he wouldn't write off the elk—he'd take some of them out at his next opportunity, damn varmints that they were.

Once the pain pills had kicked in and the other medications had calmed the surging of his stomach, Jack was ready to take on the world again. He planted his hat on his head, shaped its brim over his eyes, and swaggered out to check on the one employee still at hand. Then on the way to the stock barn Jack stopped at the corral to watch the horses for awhile. He never felt more comfortable than leaning, one foot kicked up on the bottom rail and both arms dangling over the top rail, on a corral fence. Chuck had the rest of the remuda with him and the boys on the Rim, but there were still three mares and a gelding to watch.

Pepper, a little quarter horse that'd been around forever, wandered over to give Jack's hand a sniff, then he stretched his neck to chew at the tufts of grass beyond the fence line. That made Summer curious, and as she moved closer the two younger mares followed. Soon Jack had a crowd gathered and that automatically set him to talking:

"Ladies, ladies, take your turn," he said, as they crowded the fence, looking for handouts. "You're still a pretty little girl, aren't you, Summer?" The big dun mare nodded her head agreeably while Maggie—"the nag," as Jack thought of her—pushed closer to Jack with her nose out. "Sorry, Maggie, but you're not likely to win any beauty contests, no way, no sir. And you, Pepper, you damn scavenger. You're too damn stringy for dog meat, and you know it."

Jack had ridden Pepper right into the ground one miserable winter, trying to save the herd from a long, hard freeze that'd choked the stock tanks with a thick layer of ice and buried their feed under several feet of snow. They'd started out before sunrise and traipsed up one canyon and down another, trying to push all the cattle they could find to where they'd unloaded the hay behind a windbreak of juniper, not stopping for lunch, not stopping to even let the horse blow. Jack had hopped off of Pepper literally as he'd dropped, leaving the gelding on its side in the snow, its labored breath sending up white puffs of steam like pipe smoke. Then he'd trudged the last half-mile to the portable corral they'd set up near the stock tank that had been axed clear of ice, climbed another horse in his string, and kept on working,

The gelding had drug himself off somewhere by the time Jack had returned to look for him, and it had taken Pepper another whole day to stagger on his own back to the ranch, and then another month for him to get his head up out of the dirt, but he'd toughed it out. Now he was too old to ride, too bony to even sit on, but nothing would stop Jack from feeding and caring for him. He'd have to drop again, and this time he'd have to stay down before Jack would give him up.

Hud must have noticed the commotion at the corral from the house because he came wagging up, fawning at Jack's knees. Jack knew what he wanted—anytime Jack went near a horse, Hud was on the spot. Even though he would come back now with his tongue hanging half out of his head, limping, a good run was still Hud's idea of heaven. But Jack's daughter was right—he hadn't been in any shape to go bouncing through the sage brush in years, although he still had not officially admitted it, even to himself.

"You stupid dog," he told Hud. "You think I don't have nothin' better to do than run you all over creation?" But he did allow the dog to follow him over to the stock barn where Jack could get out of the sun and even lie down on the cot in the tack room, if he wanted to, without anybody bothering him.

Fred was sitting in the open breezeway of the barn, mending a bridle, as Jack walked in. The old Mexican bit off the end of the thick thread he was working with and nodded to Jack, all in one motion. Fred was the only Hispanic on the place, and he'd been around so long Jack forgot to think of him as one of the "greasers" he so adamantly refused to hire.

More and more of the ranches in the west were being run with Mexican labor, now that it was so difficult to find Americans who were willing to earn a wage with their own sweat. Jack had heard of a rancher who'd gone all the way to Peru to find enough cowboys to work his spread. But all this talk in the Brown Barn Saloon about how cowboying was a dying lifestyle had only made Jack more obstinate. He'd already hired kids from the college in Flagstaff who were so green they lost their breakfast at the sight of a calf's castration, and if he had to, he'd hire the drunks off the streets of Winslow, long as they could stay on a horse during roundup, before he'd let a damn "*vaquero*" on his place.

Except for Fred, of course, who'd been eating at Jack's table since Jack Senior had hired him on when Jack and Fred were both teenagers. Fred had always been pretty closed-mouth about his past—in fact, Fred seldom had much to say about anything, although he'd answer a direct question readily enough—but he'd had enough English when he walked up the drive to the ranch, a worn-out Levi jacket his only protection from a ripping November wind, to talk Jack's father into giving him a job mucking the stalls that winter.

From then on, Fred was a fixture around the place. He helped out quite a bit during calving and branding, but the rest of the year he pretty much stayed in the barn with the horses, right up until mealtime, when he'd show up in a clean shirt, his hair—thinning now, but still black as a fire pit—slicked back and neatly parted. He ate whatever Katie set in front of him, and no matter what went on at the table around him, as soon as he was finished Fred stood up, gave Katie a little bow, thanked her for his dinner, and made his way out the screen door and back to the barn or over to the bunkhouse.

Jack lowered himself onto the bench outside an empty stall and watched Hud go sniffing up and down the breezeway like he thought he'd missed something during the night. Fred had finished his task and sat with the bridle over one knee, his hands in his lap, staring out the open doorway to where Mount Humphrey rose, distant and silver-backed, over the mesa.

"Too hot today," he said finally. "We're going to be feeding those steers cactus again afor this summer's over."

Jack snorted and leaned back against the stall, not thinking about the ranch at all, not the damn weather that had tormented him all his life, not the stock or the men or his daughter, whose lives all depended on him. He let his chin fall to his chest and closed his eyes.

SIX

Richard had opened the door for me. He'd already pushed his way into the Walgreens, but then he backed up against the glass door again so I could come in after him, and he smiled at me as I passed. He smiled really sweetly, even though he must have known I was Jack Rawlings' daughter. I certainly knew who Richard was, as my father would still occasionally launch into a tirade about this "new" social studies teacher, months after their association on the school board had ended. And he didn't even seem to mind that I took my time walking into the cool of the store, staring past the thick, black glasses to see if his eyes really were as beady and cunning as Dad had said. They weren't, of course. His eyes, I decided, turning away with sudden embarrassment, looked kind.

I think he was sick that day because while I was scouting magazines, stocking up on shampoo and antiperspirant, he was back at the pharmacist's window waiting for an order to be filled. I felt a little like Red Riding Hood with the handles of that plastic shopping basket cutting into the crook of my arm, weaving through the store aisles even though I'd finished shopping, scoping out the big, bad wolf. By then I'd decided he was attractive, with long legs but a longer torso and a boy's narrow waist and shoulders. His black hair curled below his collar—long for our town—and he still wore that bristly mustache I made him shave off after our second date.

The first date barely qualifies, but I call it that, since if we hadn't met again at the Thunderbird Cafe a few days later and started talking over coffee, he would never have glimpsed the woman I'd been sheltering for so many years, and he would never have asked me out for the "real" date that he thinks was our first.

Sharon had leaned over the counter—she's the reason I used to frequent the Thunderbird, a woman in her fifties, with crayoned-in red lips and a bust, worthy of the name, that threatened to explode from the confines of her waitress uniform—and remarked, loud enough for him to hear: "Mr. Crawford likes his coffee almost as much as you do, hon. If you two would sit a little closer, I could keep both those cups full without walkin' my tail off."

I don't think I had even known he was there until she said that. I always sat at the counter so I could talk with Sharon in her pauses between placing an order, making the drinks and sides, and running it all to a table. I was hunched over the counter, blowing on my coffee, waiting for Sharon to stop for a second with her hands on her hips and make a remark to me or to take a few drags from the cigarette she left smoking in the ashtray in front of me. I would answer her every comment, trying to be wise and sassy like her, knowledgeable in the ways of the world—even though I wasn't. Maybe she wasn't, either. She died last year of lung cancer.

So I twisted around to look over my shoulder, and he was in a booth by the cash register, his hands up like he was waiting to catch something. Me, I guess. I must have been feeling really brave that day because instead of just blushing and hanging my head like I normally would I took Sharon's nudge to heart and stood up. I carried my coffee over and he half-rose—you know how some men do when a lady starts to sit down—gesturing toward the other seat at the booth like I couldn't see for myself which side to sit on. So I sat. Then I put my hands in my lap and waited.

We didn't *have* to talk. Richard had the newspaper opened on the table, and he could have just kept reading, grunting every now and then to show how interesting an article was, and Sharon would have swished up, filled both cups, frowned and swished away again all morning. But he folded the paper and put it away, fixing those eyes on *me*, instead—they were blue, I realized this time, with long, black lashes, hidden behind Coke-bottle lenses and stern, black frames. He asked me my name, first, but like he knew it ("You're Katherine Rawlings, right?") and introduced himself, like I didn't know his ("Rich Crawford—I teach at the high school, or rather, I try to."). Did I laugh? I think I did.

But still I kept my head turned to the window as if there was something really interesting going on out there in the parking lot.

He tried asking me questions for a while ("So, do you work here in town at all?"). Hah! I think that's how I really answered him. No. My father would never . . . . ("Just doing a little shopping, then?") Maybe, although needing something that couldn't be raised, made or done without was just the excuse. I escaped to town at least twice a week to reassure myself that the world was populated with creatures that didn't stink, neigh, moo or bark. I did tell him I volunteered at the public library on Tuesday afternoons. ("That's great!" he said.) Would he have been so enthusiastic if he'd known all I did was type up index cards for a mismanaged catalogue?

When it sunk in how shy I was he took over, telling me he was from Flagstaff and had taught there for almost ten years, before moving down to Phoenix to get his MBA. His family had wanted him to return to Flagstaff to run their real estate management firm, so he had, but he'd burned out after a couple years and decided to go back to his first love, his real love: teaching. It's funny; I remember he used the word "love" like that without mentioning the woman whom he had nearly married and whose death had been the real cause of his move. Instead he told me Winslow High had offered the only job he could find so late in the summer, but he'd been here two years now and was happy. The kids were unwilling to work hard at their studies, but that was true most places, these days. And they had some really troubled kids at this school—the "juvie" kids, my dad called them, wards of the state, orphans and such—and Richard had accepted an extra contract to stay after school to work with them and the in-school suspension kids. It was kind of like babysitting, he acknowledged, except none of them were babies and not a whole lot of sitting went on.

When Sharon came by to refill our cups she did something wonderful—she winked. I'm sure both of us saw her do it because when I finally looked up, reaching for the milk to pour in my coffee, I saw

Richard was just raising his head, too. We smiled our embarrassment across the table at each other, and right then I knew that I had found my version of Faulkner's Homer Barron, the man I would try to poison with a whole life's worth of frustrated love.

SEVEN

This time the cops picked me up at the Flagstaff bus station where I'd been bumming change for Cheez-Its and crap like that from the snack machine, trying to figure out how to make it to the West Coast somehow, and I was cold and hungry enough by then—all I had was the clothes I'd been wearing when I'd taken off—to let them haul me down to the station without a fuss; they gave me a pukey-smelling blanket and bought me a hamburger on the way. But I wasn't ready yet to tell them anything about who I was—which is a matter of some debate, I've discovered—or where I was goin'—which has never been a certain thing. I'd messed up pretty bad this time, so it wasn't really a surprise to me that they couldn't find any missing persons report that matched my description. I guess it's kind of like a convoluted version of the cry wolf story—if you keep runnin' away enough times, finally they'll just let you keep on going.

It was the lady from Child Protective Services who suggested I try for the emancipated minor thing, after I gave her an earful of mostly but not entirely invented crap about Lily. Then I found out to do that I would have to file a petition in the family court in the right jurisdiction, and no way was I going back to Phoenix. Besides I'm smart enough to know with all the truancy shit I've pulled, plus getting' kicked out of school and such, I wasn't really going to be able to prove I was ready to take care of myself.

But talking to the legal aid guy is how I found out that Lily's name is on my birth certificate—the little slut! Just a "John Doe" father, of course. She would have been just a little older than I am now when she had me. I threw one of my most gargantuan fits ever when the guy told me. This one wasn't faked, either; a scream just boiled up out of me—I was so f-ing pissed off to be *lied* to about something as important as who your f-ing *mother* was for sixteen f-ing *years*. And it just kept coming, past breath, past sound, past any sense at all, and I was thrashing around at anyone stupid enough to come near me until I just got exhausted and ended up curled into a shuddering ball under the table. Scared him shitless, I can tell you that, because to get me up off the floor he agreed he'd never let on to her or anybody else that they'd found me. 'Course maybe he actually did tell her and she just didn't do nothin' about it. I realize that's perfectly possible.

They've got this special program at the high school here in Winslow for troubled kids, so that's where they sent me. For the first couple of weeks I was, like, stunned. I kind of shut down and just went through the motions of going to school and eating and all that stuff, you know, just did what I was told. I didn't run because I didn't know which way to go. I'd killed the only thing I loved right before I left Cave Creek—a beautiful black stallion, an Arabian, worth a fortune—and doing that had surely lost me forever the only person I cared about—and who had really cared about me, despite all his deceits and denials. There's no way in hell Guy could ever be able to forgive me for drowning that horse. I know that for certain. I know it because I will never forgive myself.

EIGHT

Spider Woman had instructed them to stare down their enemies without flinching; she'd said to shake the sacred eagle feather charm at them and sing their magic song AS LOUD AS THEY COULD. Doing so had gotten them past the rocks, the sharp-as-spears reeds, the spines, and even across the scorching sand dunes, and each travail had made the boys more confident. But now they stood before Sun's turquoise house.

"We have done well to arrive in one piece here," said White Shell Woman's son. "I do expect a trick, though. We can't just walk in there."

But Changing Woman's son responded: "Surely a father will welcome a son's visit, even if he didn't invite him." He stepped through the door and surprised the woman inside by proclaiming, "We were told by Spider Woman to come see our father the Sun! We seek his help!"

The other boy stepped inside, as well, and both boys stood up very straight in the center of the room.

The woman wiped her hands on her skirt, regarding them. "He's your father you say?" she asked them, eyes narrowing. "And why is it then that I am not your mother?"

From that they boys realized they were speaking to Sun's wife. One toed the dirt floor, the other raised his eyes to the ceiling. Finally Changing Woman's son cleared his throat and repeated: "We need our father's help. There are monsters devouring our people, and we seek the means to destroy them."

The woman put her hands on her hips and grunted in response. The day was waning; she needed to act fast if she was going to help them. She knew her husband's unthinking reaction to seeing strangers in his home when he returned from his travels across the sky would be to slaughter them. "Lie down there on that blanket," she told them, "and roll yourselves up. Do not make any noise; do not speak or cough or sneeze. Your very lives depend on this."

The boys looked at one another and then scrambled to do as she'd instructed. Already they could hear the pounding footsteps of someone approaching, and by the time they'd pulled the dusty blanket over their heads and rolled into a corner they heard the rattle over the door shake as someone stomped into the chamber. Then the room was filled with heat; light penetrated even the thick weave of the blanket. They heard the clang of metal as Sun hung his glowing shield up on the west wall of the house and then his booming voice asking, "Where are they? As I was crossing the sky today I saw two young men approaching, and now it seems that you have hidden them from me. What am I to think, woman?"

"What indeed," Sun's wife responded angrily. "It is you who must explain yourself. Two very handsome young men truly did come to visit me today. Unfortunately they were looking for *you*, not me, for Spider Woman had told them you are their father. How could this be, husband, when again and again you've assured me that you stay away from all the creatures of the surface world? If I am the only woman you lay with, whose sons are these?"

Suddenly the boys felt the blanket being pulled away. Changing Woman's son tried desperately to hold on to it but he was not strong enough; White Shell Woman's son let out a mighty sneeze. Then both boys sat blinking in their father's light.

NINE

Jack came to with a start, his heart pounding. He wiped the saliva from his bristled chin and heard again the stallion's scream that had awakened him. Jack could hear Hud barking excitedly and Fred's chair was empty; something was wrong. He rose to his feet with a groan, steadied himself against the stall door, then hobbled, blinking, into the noon-bright yard.

Fred only lapsed into Spanish in moments of extreme distress or excitement—that time during branding when he'd been the target of a momma cow's revenge, for instance, and Chuck had been laughing too hard to get a rope over the she-devil's head. But Jack could hear a steady stream of *Español* coming from the side corral now. He followed the sound, pulling his hat down, squinting and still half-blind in the glare, past the front paddock where the other horses were churning up the dust, racing back and forth along the fence and whinnying in response to the stallion's anxious calls.

Fred was partially obscured in his own cloud of dust, then Jack watched the stallion—Midnight, they called him, a big black, with the thick haunches of a quarter horse but the height and neck of his thoroughbred dam—rising up out of the cloud to claw the air over the small figure of the man.

Fred switched to English when he caught sight of Jack. "Get a rope, get a rope," he yelled. Fred was back-tracking as the stallion reared, then climbing hand-over-hand up the lead line, struggling to hang on as the big black charged at the fence, wheeled, and reared again.

Jack looked stupidly at the posts and ground around the corral; the nearest rope was back in the tack room. He heard Richard come puffing up behind him and whirled around: "Get a rope, damn it!" he barked at his son-in-law, then they both watched, slack-jawed, as the stallion hurled himself over the bars of the corral and landed hard a few feet away from them. The shock knocked the stallion's legs out from under him and he fell with a thud on his broad chest, but then he was scrambling up, snorting and bug-eyed, and racing toward the front corral, the lead line snaking along behind him. Fred had been yanked against the fence—he was gripping his shoulder, his face twisted into a grimace—but Jack turned away from his slow-motion drop into the dirt to watch the stallion take the second fence like a world-class jumper, haunches coiled then extended, his back hooves barely grazing the top rail. He immediately charged one of the mares.

When Jack looked back he saw that Richard had climbed between the poles of the side corral and was kneeling on the ground beside Fred, then helping the older man slowly to his feet. Fred's face was a strained white, streaked with mud where the sweat was running, and he was cradling his left arm across his chest. But he wasn't flopping around like a fish on the ground from a dislocated shoulder, so Jack figured Richard could handle the necessary first aid. He spit the dirt out of his mouth and went to watch the inevitable take place in the front paddock.

Jack knew he was going to catch hell for this. Katie had told him he was crazy bringing a stallion onto the place—she'd been downright crude about it, saying the last thing they needed was another stud to feed, and implying Jack's motives had more to do with his own failing *machismo* than any need for foals. Jack had shouted her down, as usual, but the barb had dug in deep enough to trouble him now.

And it was true, Ol' Midnight had been a pain in the ass from day one. Chuck was the only one on the place who was any good at handling the brute, and if he was busy on a round up or just didn't get around to exercising him one day, the stallion would pound the hell out of the walls of his stall all night, and by morning, sparks would be shooting out of his eyes and he'd be snorting fire. And now, in addition to his feed and vet bills, there'd be Fred's trip to the doctor's to pay for. And for what? Summer had been a good brood mare in her time, but now she was one of the oldest mares on the place. The poor girl would be hard pressed to produce a healthy foal from this.

Summer was putting up a good fight at the moment, launching powerful kicks at the stallion's nose and dashing away, then turning with her teeth bared when the stallion pursued her. But there was nowhere for her to run, really; she'd charge a fence, rear, shrieking, and box the air, churning up a veil of dust that shrouded the forms of the horses as if nature was ashamed of the drama that was unfolding. The stud just kept pressing his case until he wore the mare down. She finally gave up kicking and submitted, wide-eyed and quivering, to his mount.

The other horses were clumped at the far end of the corral, huddled together like the helpless witnesses of a rape. The sound effects alone were terrifying; the stallion was wheezing violently, drowning out the mare's protests with his grunting. Blood was running down the side of Summer's neck from the bites he'd inflicted while subduing her. Then suddenly it was over; the stud slid off her back and went back to grazing along the fence line, the picture of indifference. Summer shook herself and then stood with her nose in the dirt.

Jack jumped at the sound of Richard's voice. "That bastard," he said as he jerked open the corral gate. "Fred says he had no idea Summer was in estrus, but that son-of-a-bitch sniffed her out in no time." The clutch of horses swirled to keep their distance as Richard strode through the corral. "Whoa, you stupid shit," he commanded the stallion. Jack couldn't help smiling at his son-in-law's temper. Midnight raised his head but allowed Richard to catch his halter rope and turn him toward the gate.

Jack looked back at the car and swallowed his grin; Katie was standing beside Fred, who was hunched over in the passenger's seat. He met Richard at the gate and took Midnight's halter. "You better get Fred in to the doc," Jack said. "I'll see to this." When Richard hesitated, glancing toward the car, Jack yanked at the lead to make the horse step forward. "Go on," he insisted. "And take Kate with you. She'll feel a damn sight better if she's there to hold Fred's hand."

On the way to the barn Jack heard the car start up, but he was disappointed, looking back over his shoulder, to see that his daughter had not gone along and was standing in the middle of the dusty yard, her hands on her hips, her belly making a tent of her dress, watching him.

Jack got Midnight into his stall with no problems; he was mild as a carrot, now, and it was hard to imagine he was the same horse that had been terrorizing the place only moments ago. Hud came wagging up, his tongue hanging out and still smiling from all the excitement, while Jack checked the stallion out for damages. The mare had clipped him a few times in the chest and planted a couple bites of her own; Jack got the Bag Balm out and salved the wounds after wiping the crust of blood and dirt off with a towel.

Then he went back outside and found Summer rolling on her back in the dirt, stirring up a cloud of dust. He just stood by and watched; she was a mess, with blood matted on her neck and flanks, but the thought of going in there and catching her, haltering her and hosing her down—it was all too much. The ache in his gut had kicked in again. It had nothing to do with hunger, but Jack decided he needed to eat anyway. He hitched up his pants and crossed the yard, Hud following at his heels, and climbed up the steps to the house.

From the hallway he could see that Katie had made a sandwich for him and left it sitting on the kitchen table, but when he held his breath, listening for her, and didn't hear anything, he crept over to the gun case on the living room wall instead of going in to eat. Just for fun he tried the bicycle lock, tested a few combinations, then yanked and swore at it. Just one time—one time—he had taken down a shot gun, loaded it, released the safety, and taken it out on the porch with him to scare off a Game and Fish bureaucrat. For that—for trying to protect his property—they had heaped this humiliation on him.

Now Jack had taken it long enough. In the unlocked drawer at the bottom of the case, under the box of shotgun shells, he found the half-empty carton of .45's. "That's my girl," he thought, emptying the bullets for Katie's little pistol into his pocket and replacing the empty box. Then he went back to his lunch, feeling like he'd accomplished quite a bit for one day, despite all the distractions.

The phone rang just as Jack was searching through the cupboards for a toothpick; he never could remember where Katie had them hidden. He heard her footsteps come heavily down the stairs, then the anxious tone of her voice as she picked up the receiver.

Jack moved over to the threshold where he could make out her words without being seen. "How bad?" he heard his daughter ask, then she tsked and sighed as she listened. "Okay, Rich," she said after a moment. "Well, do what you think is best." That got to Jack—why the hell would she want to let Richard do her thinking for her? "Oh, and Rich, make sure to talk to Doc Levy about Dad. I need to know what else I should be doing. Okay. I know. I will." Then Katie was finishing up her conversation and Jack had to hurry back to the kitchen table and sit down.

"Fred's arm is broken above the elbow," she announced as she entered the room. "It's just a hair-line fracture, but they're putting a cast on it from his armpit to his wrist."

Katie took a glass down from the cupboard and filled it with water at the sink; Jack watched her drink it, thinking how bad she looked—puffy-faced and her hair all tousled.

"Poor Alfredo," she said, staring out the window. Then she refilled her glass and brought it over to the table with her. "Richard says he's going to call some of the kids from his school—see if he can get one of them to come out and help for a while."

"What?" Jack exploded. So this was his son-in-law's brilliant idea. "I'll be damned if I'll give some snot-nosed delinquent the run of this place."

Katie groaned as she lowered herself onto a chair.

"You just call him back, you hear me? Tell him he can forget that idea."

"What else are we going to do, Dad?" she asked tiredly, looking down into her glass. "We've been short-handed for a long time, now. Fred's been hard put just to keep up with the horses. And now. . . ."

"Well, I'll be god-damned." Jack gathered all his outrage and faced it toward his daughter. "The poor guy gets a little bunged up and you're all ready to put him out to pasture."

Katie shook her head, smiling in her sad way. "I think Fred would be delighted to retire, Dad. He's not like you." Jack had to restrain himself from spitting on the floor—that's how violently he disagreed with her. But Katie went on like she didn't even notice. "I just wish we could afford it." She sipped her water, then leaned back, brushing her hair off her forehead. "I'd love to give him a nice fat check and send him home to his family."

This was too much for Jack. He grabbed the table with both hands and shook it. "Fred ain't got no family," he said angrily. Then he corrected himself: "*We're* his family."

Katie looked at him with that long-suffering expression that drove Jack wild. "I mean his real family, Dad—his sisters in Hermosillo and all those nieces and nephews. You just don't like admitting he's got a whole other life that has nothing to do with you."

Jack's knuckles on the table had gone white. His daughter had a hell of a nerve trying to tell him anything about a man he had spent most of his life with.

Katie had to use both hands to push herself out of her chair. She picked up Jack's empty plate and her glass and returned to the sink. "Sometimes I wish you'd get sick of this old place and let us all retire." She turned to face him, wiping her hands on a dish towel. "Ranchin's not what it used to be, Dad. And none of it's your fault—things are just different than they were in your grandpa's day. I know you still love living out here, but sooner or later it seems like we're going to have to sell and move into town."

Jack found himself rising. He had known for months that his daughter wanted to sell the ranch—she and her husband had made countless allusions to the idea, over his nodding head around the television at night, behind their bedroom door. But always—always—Katie had ended up sighing and saying how she knew he would never agree to it. And now she had actually said the words to his face.

Jack's stomach made a noise so loud he was sure his daughter had heard it. But he swallowed back the acid and said nothing. "What if something happened to you, Dad?" she asked, looking up at him dolefully. "It's at least a thirty minute drive to the hospital from here—what if, you know, you got really bad all of a sudden?"

But Jack let the stiffness of his back be her answer as he strode down the hallway and slammed out the screen door.

TEN

Alfredo would steady me on the old sorrel nag we called Katrina, telling me, "Hold on tight, *muchacha. No tengas miedo.* It's okay. The horse will never hurt you—*ella tiene tu nombre,* my little Kate." And I would hold on, my child-body stiff with terror, afraid of falling, afraid of the huge, dusty beast, screeching if Katrina turned her head, since I was convinced she wanted to bite me, although she never did.

We must have circled that corral a thousand times, the plodding, toe-dragging mare as patient as the man who held her halter and braced my side or patted my knee reassuringly. When Fred finally relented and the dreaded riding lesson was over for another day, I'd hug his neck as he helped me down, giddy with relief, gasp, "*Mucho gracias, Tio* Fred," then duck through the fence rails and race for the safety of the house.

My father could never understand it. A rancher's daughter, afraid of horses? Afraid of the wranglers' rough laughter and weathered faces? Afraid of cows, for Christ's sake? At branding time it would all converge—the loud and sweating men, the stink of burned hair and flesh and manure, the biting flies and bawling calves. My job was to haul the water bucket around, to endure the mens' winks and gap-toothed smiles. I'd watch the Adam's apples bob in their bristle-covered throats as they emptied the dipper cup but I would never speak to them—and I would never look them in the eye.

"Rabbit," they called me. "Come on over here, little rabbit, and give a tired man a drink." Fred would turn around to see if I'd heard—I always stood behind him, hiding, or helping him tend the campfires that heated the brands and cooked the noon meal of bacon, coffee, biscuits and beans. "*Apresúrense!*" he'd urge me, "*Ahora!*"

In the summers, Fred was often the only man on the place. Dad would spend days at a time on the range, obsessed with his fences and strays. Those were my vacations—no riding lessons, free to lounge on the couch and read all day, or eat Jello right out of the box while watching Fred cook his lunch on the bunk house stove. He'd tell me stories while he roasted the chilies necessary for every dish: *enchiladas, flautas, carne adovada* or *asada*, my eyes stinging from the spice-filled smoke.

"Your grandpa was a good man, a very good man," Fred told me countless times. "A real gentleman, *y un grande vaquero, muy valeroso.* His mother raised all her boys to be gentlemen, with nice manners, you know? Not savages like these *borrachos* your father hires.

"*Tu abuelo* loved his mother very much. He never married, you know, until after she died—out of respect. She never wanted other women in her kitchen, touching her things, so he waited. Your grandmother, the *Senora*, she waited, too. And waited, still, after the old woman died while *tu abuelo* built a new house for the *Senora* to live in. The old place—you know where I mean, little Kate, *si*? That clearing where the road turns and starts uphill, closer to the highway—he burned the *antigua casa* that was there to the ground. Out of respect, *nina*.

"Your grandfather raised me, *Katerina*, he and the *Senora*. I was just a boy when I came here, just a little English, no money. Their hearts let me in; they sat me down at their table. When the *Senora* died, I tell you the truth, little one, I cried like a baby. Only two years after your grandfather, to lose her! To be orphaned twice in one lifetime! Your father wore his uniform to the funerals, I remember. But only I cried—I cried enough for both of us, for all of us, the orphaned children."

Sometimes Fred would cry again, pealing the blackened skins off the chilies with a fork as tears drew shiny lines down his cheeks. He was not like the other men I knew, my *Tio* Fred. He was nothing like my father or any of the wranglers who came and left with the seasons. Fred was an orphan. Fred was like me.

ELEVEN

Lily named him Tristan because of how he was born. I never saw exactly how it happened and everything Guy'd had to do to save him because by then I was hiding at the back of my closet, upstairs in my room, as remorseful as I've ever been after some stupid prank I'd pulled had turned out worse than I'd intended.

All I'd been doing was snooping, messing around in the stall where Guy'd been camping out since he'd brought Tristan's mom in—her name was Lady Muscatta. I already had a monster crush on him; Guy was tall and cowboy-lean and had a square-jawed kind of handsomeness about him, and I knew he was off with my sister for the day, probably already doin' her, and it was cold. I plugged in his space heater and pulled his blanket off the bed while I poked around on the little shelf he'd rigged in there, kind of sifting through his stuff. There wasn't much, a couple *Breeders' World* magazines, a mirror, a comb, a cup with a razor in it, that sort of shit. I was standing too close to the space heater, I guess. I tossed the blanket down and ran like hell when I smelled smoke. I was twelve. Kids do stupid stuff sometimes.

By the time I crawled out from the pile of clothes I'd burrowed under and stood tip-toe at the window, the fire trucks were gone and so was Lady Muscatta, hauled off from the middle of the road to a dump somewhere, I guess. Maybe they made dog food out of her—what a f-ing stupid ass end for a million dollar Arabian. I could hear Lily's husband banging around downstairs, still crazy mad about what'd happened, so even though it was well past supper time I stayed put in my room, and I didn't even see the foal until mid-morning the next day when Guy finally left him to go to the bathroom or something.

Right away I fell in love with him—perfectly black, ears flicking, snuffling my hand. His big brown eyes seemed too big for his little head—just incredibly *cute*. I remember standing there crying, petting him and weeping like an idiot. I told him I was sorry.

I never meant to bring him in through fire. And I never meant to take him out through flood.

TWELVE

Sun growled his fury and seized a boy in each hand, then he hurled them against the eastern wall of his house. But Changing Woman's son held tight to the eagle feather charm and White Shell Woman's son was singing their magic song VERY LOUDLY; they bounced off the wall unhurt. Sun was boiling with emotion—rage, shame, even fear. He grabbed them again and slung them against his southern wall; again they slid to the ground unscathed. Now Sun was also feeling a bit confused. He tried throwing them against his western wall—splat!—but the boys scrambled to their feet again, holding their charm before them, chanting. Wonder crept into Sun's jumble of emotions. When smashing them against the northern wall also did them no harm, Sun mumbled to himself: "Whoa. Perhaps it would be good if these young men *were* my sons."

But this would not make his wife very happy, so Sun tried a new strategy to get rid of them. "So—we've got the dust off. Now I'd like you to join me in my sweathouse," he said with a false smile. He would cook them alive in there!

The boys feared treachery, but what could they do but stumble out of the house and across the yard to the sweathouse? Sun lifted the hide cover over the door, tossed in hot boulders from his wife's cooking fire, and ushered the boy's inside. Immediately their eyes burned, their skin sizzled, their hair started to smoke. The boys dropped to the ground, crept to the edge of the lodge and pressed their flush faces to the crack of light at its base; there they could breathe and even find enough wind to answer their father's hollered question: "Is it hot enough?"

"Yes, Father!" they shouted back in unison.

Suddenly a downpour of water came in from the roof and a cloud of hissing steam filled the room. "Is it hotter still?" the Sun asked, hoping he would not get an answer.

But the boys gulped air through the chinks in the wall and answered politely, "Yes, it is really, really hot in here!"

Sun was amazed. He lifted the cover over the door and peered inside. "I guess you *must* be my children," he said to them, pride finally edging out all the other feelings. "You are strong young men. You endure hardship very well. You must tell me what it is that you need from me."

THIRTEEN

Jack was standing in the kitchen of the trailer swallowing pills as Richard's car crept down the driveway. He shook his head as he watched his son-in-law hurry around the front of the car to open Fred's door and then spat in the sink at the solicitous way Richard eased the older man from the passenger's seat and hollered at Hud to get out from underfoot. Fred's leathery face looked washed-out—even from this distance—but regardless, the doting way Richard led him toward the bunkhouse made Jack's stomach turn. Katie came out of the house and trailed after them, her head down, supporting the sides of her belly with her hands as she walked.

Jack turned around with a sigh. He dumped the bullets out of his pocket onto the rickety wooden table, then he went over to the couch to dig the pistol out from under the cushion. He sat down at the table to load the gun, sighted at the water tank through the window, then spun the barrel, listening to the clicks of the chambers. He weighed the loaded gun in the palm of his hand.

He had never thought about turning a weapon on himself before, so the idea struck him as something new and stimulating. The tingle started at the base of his skull and spread across his shoulders. He considered where he would plant the bullet—would he put the barrel in his mouth or rest the cool steel against a temple? Then he thought about Katie hearing the report and rushing to the trailer.

Jack had seen the effects of a .45 at close range; he'd been nine or ten-years-old, standing behind his father's chair during a poker game in a Winslow saloon that had long since burned down, when the drunk cowboy beside his father had accused the man opposite them of cheating.

Jack's father had used the incident as a lesson on poker etiquette: "Leave your cards on the table when you're playing stud," he'd told Jack later. This man had held his "down" cards in his lap one too many times; in the middle of the next hand the drunk cowboy's whole body had stiffened. Jack had leaned closer, assuming it was something good—a full house, perhaps. Then the next minute a bullet shot up through the table and pierced the other man's throat.

Blood had pumped out through the man's fingers; it came in surges, just like a stunned and throat-slit steer. Jack had watched, fascinated, until his father dragged him through the crush of people and out into the dark street. Jack remembered the sound of his father retching into the gutter, then they'd driven home in silence.

He knew now why his father had puked. When Jack was a boy, death had been impossible. Even as a grown man, Jack had never really believed in it. He'd survived the broken bones from fingers twisted into lariats and horses falling on him, the frostbite and exposure, all the truck accidents, without ever worrying about an end to his life. But now the gun was loaded and in his hand.

The sound of footsteps on the trailer steps startled him so much he nearly dropped it. He lurched out of the chair and stood in the middle of the kitchen, moving the pistol guiltily from hand to hand, then he slid it into the silverware drawer just as someone rapped on the metal door.

"Dad?" Katie called. She opened the door and stuck her head inside. "Fred's back," she said when she saw him. "Why don't you come and talk to him? He's feeling pretty bad about what happened."

Jack just grunted at her and waved her away. He went over to the couch and sat down, then stretched out with his hands folded across his chest.

"Oh, Dad," he heard Katie say plaintively, but he kept his eyes closed until the trailer door rattled shut. Then he meant to get up but he didn't.

Dreaming, Jack was back on horseback, moving with the fluid grace of his youth, the power of the beast rising up through the strong grip of his legs. The same old cowboy had taught both him and Fred everything they knew about riding and roping, the basics of their trade.

They'd called him Sammy Red for the blush that crawled up his face every time he spoke to another person, stranger or familiar, it didn't make any difference. As teenagers they'd spent most of their summers in the stock corral with Sammy, breaking in the colts and fillies or working the older horses, getting them ready for the rigors of fall roundup.

Sammy was a great believer in the superiority of animals over most of humankind. When a green horse bucked it was their fault; a mare that didn't back and plant her legs just at the moment when the rope grew taunt, or swing to the right at the first nudge of their heel, was an inexcusable failure on their part.

Fred would get disheartened by the criticism and find some work back in the barn that he had to do. Jack ate it up like candy. He admired the gimpy old cowboy—a shattered hip made him limp on the ground but he still moved smooth as twelve-year-old scotch on horseback—almost as much as he worshipped his old man.

In his dream, Sammy was sitting on the corral fence, repeating something over and over. Jack would float by on his horse and catch a few words of it, then he'd leave the old man jabbering in his dust. What was he supposed to hold on to? That wasn't clear to Jack at all. And who had gone to get help? Why? When Jack looked down he realized it was Midnight's black withers moving under him.

The buzzing of flies brought Jack around. He waved one away from his face and sat up on the couch, then watched a bunch of them banging against the sunny window on the west side of the trailer. He got up slowly, pulling at his wet shirt, then he went outside and urinated off the steps of the trailer. He was still groggy with sleep and heat as he shut the door behind him and started walking toward the barn. About half-way there he remembered that Fred had got his arm broke and angled over toward the bunkhouse.

When Jack Senior had built the mud-brick and wooden structure to house his hired hands they'd had half a dozen men living on the ranch full time, over twice that during round-ups and branding. Some of the plaster was wearing off the exterior, but the low-slung walls, faced with a long verandah, were still solid. The building was split in two parts, with the kitchen separated from the men's sleeping quarters by a narrow alleyway, and windows and doors on opposing walls to create the best breeze, in the Texas style of Grandpa Jack's boyhood.

Now Fred was the only permanent resident. Except when the day's work required an especially early start, the other hands preferred to stay in town. The cow boss, Chuck, was married to one of the waitresses at the Thunderbird Inn in Winslow, and he had two kids and a house just down the street from the restaurant. Tom stayed at his girlfriend's place, and Jack had no idea where Jimmy went to, but he was always the first one to leave the ranch and the last one back in the morning.

Jack stopped in the shade of the weathered porch and wiped the sweat off his forehead—he'd left his hat somewhere—and debated whether to go inside or not. He hated sickness, had never had any patience with the infirm; he'd avoided his own wife during most of her illness. But when he stuck his head inside he saw that Fred was sitting in a chair, at least, his feet up on the old wood stove in the center of the room. Bunks with thin, rolled-up mattresses still lined the far wall, but Fred's bed was to the right of the door, next to a little pantry he'd rigged up out of bricks and boards.

Jack cleared his throat and watched Fred's head bob against his chest for a moment, then it rolled up and Fred opened heavy-lidded eyes. He took his feet down off the stove and, grimacing, sat up in the chair.

"Well, you're a picture," Jack growled. "I guess we'd better change the sign out front to Sunset Nursing Home."

Fred just looked uncomfortable and touched his cast with the fingertips of his good hand. It ran the length of his arm, from shoulder to wrist, making a sharp right angle at his elbow.

"I s'pose you'll be wanting a nurse now, huh?" Jack leaned against the door frame with his thumbs in his front pockets.

"No." Fred shook his head and tried to smile. "Nurses aren't so good with horses." Then he looked up at Jack with his head tilted.

"Ah, Jesus," Jack sighed. There was a wind-up alarm clock ticking away on the crate beside Fred's bed—Jack wondered how the man could sleep with all that racket right by his head. He pushed himself off the doorjamb, hitched up his jeans, and stood uneasily in the middle of the room.

"Grab a chair," Fred urged him.

"Naw, I just come by. . . ." But Jack looked around for the other wooden chair and ended up pulling it over and easing himself down onto it.

Jack had never noticed the deep creases that lined Fred's face; one gutted his forehead, others gathered around each eye and hollowed out his cheeks. "I tell you what, though," Fred was saying, "I could use some help in the barn for a while. Like Richard said, you know—get a kid in here."

Jack rubbed the whiskers on his chin and made a long face.

"It wouldn't be permanent, just, you know . . . . Six weeks, the Doc said, and I'll be good as new."

Jack scowled, thinking about how much he hated that damn doctor. He'd sat right across from Jack, saying things that would have reduced a weaker man to tears, but just as calm and nice as you please, with his soft hands folded on his fine wooden desk.

"And I'd keep my eye on the kid, you know that." Fred winced and adjusted his arm. "I don't see any other choice, Jack, unless, well, if you wanted to sell some of the stock now . . . ."

"Ah, to hell with it," Jack roared. He was halfway to the door before he realized he'd stood up, and he was pulling on the handle before he knew what he was going to do next. It wasn't until he was looking across the yard to the house that he decided he was going to have a little talk with his son-in-law.

Hud was lying in the square of shade that the low sun had left on the east end of the porch, and he rolled onto his back when Jack stomped up the steps, dusting the weathered wood boards with his tail. Jack paid him no mind. He wrenched open the screen door and was immediately sorry that he hadn't stopped to knock or peer inside.

Katie was lying down on the couch, her feet elevated on pillows and a cloth folded on her forehead. Richard was perched beside her, leaning down, speaking in a soothing voice, his hand spread on the top of Katie's distended belly like snow-cap on a mountain. Kate pulled the wash rag off her head and got up on her elbows when she heard him come in; Richard just glanced at him over his shoulder.

"Dad?" she said, "Is something wrong?"

"Hell, yes, there's somethin' wrong," Jack answered. He'd already taken a step backwards, but he knew it was too late to beat a retreat, so he squared his shoulders and hitched his thumbs through his belt loops. "I'd like to have a few words with your husband," he announced. That got Richard to turn around, at least. Katie dropped her head back down and started massaging her temples. The girl must have a headache, Jack reasoned. "In private," he added, although he wasn't rightly sure what he would say yet, or why his daughter couldn't hear it.

Katie sat up then, her shoulders curved in like folded wings; her whole body seemed to hunch over the mound of her belly. Then she raised her head to look from her husband to Jack. "Dad," she began, but Jack interrupted her.

"You go on," he told his daughter, jerking his chin at the stairs. Maybe all he really wanted was for her to lie down for awhile and then come back downstairs looking like she felt better, or like she'd at least gotten some sleep.

But the girl wasn't having any of it. She heaved herself up off the couch—Richard had to get up, too, and help lift her with a hand under her elbow—and started toward him, the color rising in her cheeks. "You don't talk to me at all for days at a time," she fumed—her fingers were spread like she intended to reach out and throttle him, and Jack took another step back—"then when you finally *do* have something to say, you think you can just send me upstairs? You think I'm still your little kid? You think I can't handle it? What?" Her voice had risen to a high-pitched squeak by the time she stood in front of him, her belly only inches from his own.

"Kate," Richard said. That's all he said. Then when the girl turned to look at him he just dipped his head toward the stairs. She gave Jack a final withering look and turned away, groaning with frustration.

Jack watched her climb the stairs, one hand on the railing and the other on her hip, stopping every four or five steps, until she made it to the top. Then he turned back to look at his son-in-law with a mixture of admiration and contempt.

The son-of-a-bitch's hair was too long, hanging in loose curls around the open collar of his shirt, but Jack had long since given up on the faggot jokes to get him to cut it. Besides, the younger man stood a whole head taller than Jack, and showed some evidence of a temper—like now, when he turned from watching his wife ascend the stairs and bumped Jack aside on his way to the kitchen.

Jack followed him, then watched Richard take a juice glass out of one cupboard and the whiskey bottle out of another. Richard poured himself a generous shot and knocked it back.

Jack cleared his throat. "A little early for that, ain't it?" he asked, although Jack had usually started on his own six-pack by this time of day.

"Not today, it isn't," Richard answered. He took the bottle over to the kitchen table and poured himself another glassful before he pulled out a chair and sat down.

"Well, I can't let a man drink alone," Jack decided out loud. He thought maybe Richard would get up and get him a glass, but when the younger man planted both elbows on the table, Jack went to the cupboard and got one himself.

"It's not good for you, Jack," Richard muttered, and when Jack reached for the bottle Richard surprised him by holding it down. The tug-of-war was brief, but it was enough to remind Jack that, despite Richard's slender build, he was deceptively strong.

Was it only last winter when they'd had that hip-locked calf at the end of calving season? Chuck had been up two nights straight, so Jack had sent him home and he and Fred had taken over, just in time for that first-calf heifer to fall to her knees, bellowing, and roll on her side. The calf was too big and ass-backward, his feet sticking up at the night sky.

Jack and Fred had taken turns, pulling on him, one foot braced against the cow's rump, then they'd each grabbed a leg and tried yanking the calf out together, with the heifer really raising hell, now, which got Katie up out of bed to see what was going on. They were just about to saddle Maggie and hitch up a rope when Richard stumbled over, still half asleep, that curly hair all tousled. Jack was busy and didn't listen to what Katie was saying to Richard, but the next thing they all knew, Richard had grabbed the hind legs of that calf and popped it out like it was nothing, or like maybe he was dreaming about pulling the cork out of a wine bottle.

"It's the damn liquor that's killing you, Jack," Richard was saying now, his head down, not looking at him. "That and all the red meat you've been wolfing down for God knows how many years."

Jack felt the hairs on the back of his neck rising. He wasn't going to stand here and listen to this shit, but Richard kept on.

"Kate's due in a matter of weeks, and all she can think about is you. She's worried; she's really stressed out about it, and it's not good for her. It's not good for the baby, either—your grandchild, Jack." When Richard did raise his head Jack found himself wondering how long his son-in-law had hated him. "She knew you were bleeding from the rectum months ago—she does the god-damned laundry, you know.

And she knows the polyps were cancerous 'cause Doc Levy told her. She's been trying to keep you on the diet the Doc gave her, not that you're helping her any. And if you wanted to give her a tiny piece of hope you'd agree to the treatment."

Jack had to brace himself against the back of the kitchen chair. His medication seemed to have suddenly worn off and his stomach was reeling worse than his head. Richard pulled his hands through his hair—but why the hell is *he* so upset, Jack wondered.

"I'm trying my best, but I'm not the one she needs to talk to, Jack. She's scared of losing you." Richard took his glasses off and tossed them with a clatter onto the table. "Though I have trouble understanding why," he rubbed his eyes, "since you've shut her out all these years. But there's still time for you to be her dad."

Jack raised his fist and exploded: "Don't you call *me* 'Dad'!"

Richard sat back and stared at Jack like he was some exotic zoo animal the professor hadn't seen before. "Ah, Jesus," he said finally, replacing his glasses, and Jack knew he had given up even before Richard grabbed his glass, pushed away from the table, and disappeared back into the living room.

Jack belched loudly but it didn't make him feel any better. By God, he'd come here to have *his* say and Richard had beaten him to it. So Jack followed him into the living room, waving a gnarled finger in front of him. "Damn it, I ain't dead yet, and I wouldn't give a piss in a can for what that quack doctor says. I'm still running things around here, you hear me? And if you think you're going to bring some damn juvie kid onto this place to steal me blind, well, I'd say you've got another thing coming!"

Jack was panting. He clutched the back of the couch and watched Richard settle into the rocking chair, then lean forward to take up the newspaper that had been lying on the coffee table. "One of the youngsters in my youth program has been working around horses pretty much all her life," he said, perched on the edge of the chair. "She misses them—I think it could do her some good to work ours. And we obviously need the help."

"Oh, criminy," Jack howled, "a she-devil juvie, no less. You ain't got a brain in yer head."

But Richard wasn't looking at him. There was a big wolf spider making its way across the stones of the fireplace, and Richard crept up on it, swatted it with the folded newspaper, then knocked its flattened body off against the grate. "I already talked to her case worker," Richard said as he tossed the newspaper back onto the coffee table. "She's going to bring her around tomorrow. Why don't you let Fred decide if he thinks he can work with the girl?" Richard glanced up the stairs. "Now you'll have to excuse me so I can get dinner started. We're going to be eating late as it is." He cast a sidelong look at Jack, rose, and strode out of the room, leaving Jack standing there with his hands in his pockets.

After listening to the gurgle of his stomach for several minutes, even louder to his ears than Richard's banging around in the kitchen, Jack focused on the face staring up at him from the front page of the newspaper, underlined with spider guts. The headline read: "Secretary of the Interior, Dennis Cameron, to Visit Window Rock."

"That son-of-a-bitch," Jack fumed. "How dare he show his traitor's face in these parts?" And suddenly Jack's anger had a reason and a purpose, all at once. He appropriated Richard's glass and sank down on the couch with it, grimacing as he swallowed and stroking the stubble on his chin.

FOURTEEN

My mother died when I was almost three, in this same four-posted bed, from complications following the birth of my little brother. I have a hazy memory of her, of her eyes, mostly, which were green, like mine, and there's a handkerchief in the bottom drawer of my dresser that still smells like the violet toilet water she always wore. I wish I could say I remember how it felt to be held and rocked by her, but after she died, Dad hired people to care for me and so that older memory has been overlaid with the arms and breasts and laps of other women.

I have a few photographs. I have almost no stories. Even Alfredo just shakes his head and sighs when I ask him about her. He has told me she was "*muy bonito*," but I can see that in the pictures. He said once that she was also afraid of horses, like me. I know she was born Lucille Steadman in 1936 back in Cleveland, Ohio. I don't know why she came west, or married my father when he was already in his mid-thirties (and she was only 24), or why she had to die just four years later in her bed.

Even her body is missing. The other members of our family lie in graves clustered on a little rise of land on the old homestead, near the house my great-grandfather had built and my Grandpa Jack burned to the ground. Great-grandpa Jack and his wife, Grace, are in the center, and Grandpa Jack shares his headstone with Grandma Elizabeth. My dad's four uncles are lined up along the rickety picket fence, and there's a cast-iron cross on my Uncle George's grave—Dad's brother, who died of influenza when he was only four.

There are four or five other little mounds beside George with no markings at all. Maybe a couple of them are beloved dogs or somebody's favorite cat, but I know Grandma Elizabeth had several miscarriages and at least one still-born child. The newest grave is almost thirty years old, and it is tiny, too: "Beloved Infant Son of John and Lucille Rawlings."

So I've always pretended that my mother's body is in the earth of her garden. I stand here at this upstairs window and look down on it every day, and at least every other day I work in its rows. It's the one place on this ranch that's really mine—and my mother's. And it is thriving.

There are bramble bushes all around the quarter acre plot—blackberries, raspberries and blueberries—that I pick in the fall. In early winter I grow Brussels sprouts, broccoli and cauliflower, and the onions and carrots will last under a thick bed of straw until almost spring. Then lettuce and spinach, and early tomatoes; finally corn, squash, melons and beans in the full heat of summer.

Squatted down in the bean patch, while the sun, even in late afternoon, burns into my scalp, my back, I'm closest to her. Green beans are secretive; they are invisible to most men, hidden behind broad leaves, and hard for even a stooping woman to see. I know now to hunker down with my weight on my heels, or to sit down in the dirt when my legs start to cramp, and search the plants with my fingers, pushing deep into their shade. This is how women pray, I think, squatted down, sweating, the sweet smell of our sex mixing with the damp soil and the breath of the plant, feeling what others cannot see.

The first contraction seems to start way up under my diaphragm and work its way down to my thighs. I can still hear the men arguing downstairs, and I want to call my husband but I wait, listening past my own breathing, for a long time. There—there it is again, just a cramping, really. Nothing to worry about. Early but not terribly early. Everything's going to be fine. In fact, despite this oppressive sense of impending doom, something wonderful is about to happen.

My mother's first child didn't die, and it didn't kill her. Her first child was a girl. And she was me.

FIFTEEN

I'd saved enough change and was able to buy the Drano yesterday; there's Clorox in the laundry room. I do hope that kid at my old boarding school who told me those two things make a deadly poison was right. I mean, I may be crazy, and I may have done some really bad things in my life, but I'm not insane or destructive enough to want to do a suicide half-assed and end up a drooling idiot on oxygen or something.

I'll never get enough cash together to buy enough pills—which would be my first choice—or a gun. They keep us poor on purpose, I suppose, letting us earn just enough pocket money from doing extra chores to buy chips and candy, nothing more. I muck stalls after school and our extended day program are over. They've got a mangy little mare and an old dun gelding in one of those pre-fab aluminum sheds out behind the home, "donations" to the charity that runs this place, I guess. During my brain-on-hold phase I think my case worker must have found me out there, poking around, and once I'd admitted to her that I'd always liked horses she said she could get me paid to help out back there. I actually don't mind Paula; she's okay.

But shoveling shit and brushing their dusty hides, that's all I've gone in for. I won't ever ride again, not ever. I know about everything there is to know, I remember everything Guy taught me, about grooming, training, posting, showing off the conformation of a horse. I used to think that's what I'd do: I'd make a million and buy Frank out, kick Lily off the place, and just keep going with Guy and all our Arabians. We'd make another million on the show circuit and off stud fees. But then I killed the stud—kinda bad for business. What a stupid shithead. But it was a dumb dream anyway. Even Guy said so once.

I'm not sure why he ever trusted me. He must have known I'd fuck up, sooner rather than later. He did, though. He treated me like a normal kid, never even seemed to blame me for the crap I'd pull, the stuff one of my old shrinks called "maladaptive behaviors": breaking crap for the stupid pleasure of hearing the plastic snap, stuffing whatever with gum or glue, leaving his truck lights on to keep him home with me and away from other people, other places. Lily told him; I heard her. She said, "She can't be trusted around the horses." But Guy let me help him, anyway.

I think he did it because he loved me. I don't mean the wrap-your-arms-around-his-neck kind of love—he didn't like that. I wish I meant that kind of love. But he *did* love me some. In fact, I think he might have been the only person on the planet who ever did, though he tried to trick me in the end. Too bad for him—for trusting me, and for lying to my face. Too bad for Tristan. Too bad for everyone and everything, I guess. You really can't trust a crazy person. Even a crazy person knows that.

SIXTEEN

Sun motioned for the two boys to follow him, and even before they sat together under a tree at the far edge of the compound Changing Woman's son had started explaining: "We live under the shadow of *Yé'iitsoh*, the Big Giant. He and the other Alien Monsters are eating us up. We fear for our people, and so we have come to seek your help."

"Give us weapons," White Shell Woman's son chimed in. "We must destroy *Yé'iitsoh* and the rest of those monsters."

Sun nodded and rubbed his chin. He looked over at his house and, satisfied that his wife was too far away to hear, he leaned forward and said: "There has been talk—I am not saying this is true—that the Big Giant you speak of is also my son."

The boys exchanged a glance, then they, too, looked over their shoulders at Sun's house.

"Perhaps it is a good idea to help you," Sun went on, "if only to put these rumors to rest." With that he rose and strode back to his dwelling. He motioned for the boys to remain outside but they could hear him clanging and moving things around inside and the voice of his wife, berating him. Then Sun re-emerged with his hands full. He dropped a helmet made of flint which Changing Woman's son took up and placed upon his head. Next White Shell Woman's son stooped to pick up a heavy war shirt also made of flint; he pulled it over his shoulders. Sun dumped the rest with a clatter in the center of the yard and the boys began to arm themselves. They each sheathed a sharp stone knife and grabbed a quiver of lightning arrows, then they stood tall before their father, dressed for battle.

"Indeed you are my sons," Sun said. "And now you are also warriors."

SEVENTEEN

The sun had already sunk below the horizon when Jack banged out the screen door to escape the sounds and smells and general industry of Richard's cooking. He immediately tripped over Hud. Jack threw his hands out and caught himself against the porch railing while the dog yelped sharply, more from surprise than any injury. "Jesus," Jack gasped, straightening, too shook up to even curse the dog properly. Hud slunk down the steps anyway.

Now it was the eastern sky that showed the curved gray shadow the earth cast into space. Jack decided to pack a slicker, on the outside chance of rain, and where the hell was his hat, anyway? He gripped his aching belly and hurried to the trailer while the black dog melted into the deeper black under the house.

It was getting dark inside the trailer, too, but Jack didn't want to bother with the generator, so he felt around in the cupboard for a candle. He struck one of the safety matches from the box on the little propane stove and lit the candle—but then he couldn't find a candle holder to put it in, so Jack did his packing one-handed, the flame whipping in the draft as he dumped his cereal box of medicines into the duffel bag, threw in a change of underwear and socks, a clean shirt, and after a moment's thought, his best bolo tie from the top drawer of the dresser. His hat was hanging from the bedroom door knob; Jack groaned as he reached for it. He planted the hat on his head and looked around the little trailer in the flickering light.

He remembered his razor and hair brush—Jack wanted to look presentable for his appointment with the Secretary of the Interior—and then he nearly set one of the cushions on fire, digging around in the couch for Katie's pistol. He had dumped all the pillows and cushions on the floor before he remembered he'd hidden the gun somewhere else. He looked under the old newspapers littering the coffee table and felt around on the kitchen counter. Finally the candle light glinted off the flatware and gun metal when he yanked open the silverware drawer. Jack leaned the candle carefully against the sink faucet, then bent to wrap the pistol in the underwear already in his duffel bag and cinched it up.

He left the door slightly ajar so it wouldn't rattle, then he had to duck back behind the trailer when he saw Fred, still cradling his arm, slowly making his way up to the house. Jack waited until he heard Hud's perfunctory woof—the dog's greeting for all familiar company—then he crept down the driveway to his truck and lowered the duffel bag quietly into the bed. He looked through the window and saw Richard moving around inside the kitchen, then Fred's shadow rose against the curtains and Jack ducked and hurried around to the other side of the truck.

"There's a light on," he heard Fred say from the porch. "I'll see if he's comin.'"

"No, Alfredo, you go ahead and sit down." Jack kept his head down, listening to his son-in-law. "It'll be a while yet, and he knows to come up here if he's hungry. You're supposed to be taking it easy." They went back inside, but one of the men must have let the dog out because when Jack eased open the passenger's door and slid across the seat he saw Hud standing on the porch with his nose in the air. Jack could tell from the tense arch of Hud's tail and the way he was sniffing that he'd caught the scent of something. "Hud, come," Jack said quietly. He opened the cab door.

Hud glanced at him like he'd known Jack was there all along, then whined and sat down, staring toward the trailer.

"Damn it, get over here," Jack insisted in a harsh whisper. He knew he was risking discovery for the sake of a damn dog, but Jack was fixed on one last joy ride for the two of them.

To his surprise, Hud trotted off the porch and came up to sniff his hand. The dog whimpered again and turned in a nervous circle, really worrying over something, but Jack was wasting no more time. He grabbed Hud by the scruff of the neck and pulled. The dog went stiff-legged, resisting at first, but then he clawed both of Jack's legs to jump the rest of the way onto the seat.

The driveway had just enough slope to it that Jack could get the truck rolling with a push. He didn't start it up until they were almost to the cattle guard, and he kept the headlights off all the way to the road, feeling his way in the moonless dark. The brightest thing in his rear view mirror was a flickering light in his own trailer's window, and it made Jack realize that he'd left the candle burning. But Katie would be coming over to get him for dinner soon, and she'd see to it.

Once they hit the highway, Jack punched on the headlights and accelerated, skidding onto the blacktop. He leaned across the seat to roll Hud's window all the way down, then swerved back onto his side of the road, laughing and pounding on the steering wheel. The rolling in his gut had subsided to a dull, survivable throb. He felt rejuvenated in the wind that flapped through both Hud's ears and blasted the years away like scraps of hay out of the truck bed.

Jack barreled the twenty minute drive down the highway to the outskirts of town, hit a green light at the intersection of 87 and Main, squealed around the corner, and bounced into the parking lot beside the Brown Barn Saloon. Hud scrambled to keep his balance on the worn upholstery, then looked at Jack expectantly when he shouldered open the driver's side door. "You know they don't allow mutts in the bar," Jack told him, but he allowed the dog to follow him anyway.

Jack grabbed the duffel bag out of the bed of the truck, too. Ordinarily he wouldn't give a thought to thieves, even in this part of town, but he couldn't leave a loaded pistol lying around, and the lock was busted on the driver's door—Jack had pirouetted a little too closely around a gate post last winter, and the dent interfered with the mechanism—so he slung the bag over his shoulder and led the way through the dark parking lot.

Just as he reached the back door to the bar, a police cruiser with its siren wailing turned onto 87 and headed out of town. Something was going on, Jack decided, his hand on the door handle. Jack had met a fire engine on the same road just a minute before.

There was a row of coat hooks along the back wall, and Jack hung the duffel bag by its straps and pointed at the floor below it. Hud sat down, but the bartender noticed him as Jack walked away.

"Well, look who's here," Rusty called out. "I haven't seen that black dog of yours for ages, Jack—what gives? Hey ya, pooch."

Hud stood up, wagging, head down and grinning, but he dropped to the floor like he'd been struck when Jack swung around and glared at him. "Don't smooch at my dog," Jack said gruffly as he eased onto a bar stool and knocked on the wooden counter in front of him. Rusty drew a Budweiser from the tap. "And give me one of them doughy things you call a pretzel, too," Jack said, lifting the mug.

Jack looked around once his eyes had adjusted to the dusky light. The punk kids had possession of the pool table, as usual, and there was another noisy gang of them in one of the booths, but a couple of old-timers sat at a table under the glowing Hamm's sign that showed a cartoon bear fishing out of a boat. Stu and Hank, or Henry, or whatever-his-name was.

Jack had known the man by Hank for thirty years; he had worked behind the counter at the auto parts store. Then he'd heard someone—a lady, Jack remembered, but he didn't recall who—saying, "Henry, what do you think about this?" and "Henry, would you do that?" and Jack had been stumped about what to call the man ever since.

When people called him John, he took offense. That was his legal name, all right, same as it had been his father's and grandfather's, and it went back even farther, to a great-great uncle on his grandmother's side, the Irish side, and maybe even further back, for all Jack knew. That was the name on every legal document Jack had been served or signed and it was the name on all his medical records. It was also the name carved into a granite tombstone. It only meant trouble.

So when Jack had swallowed enough beer to get the road dust out of his throat, he went over to the older men's table and said, "Howdy, Stu," but he just nodded at Hank and sat down. Stuart smiled, showing off the gaps in his teeth. He'd been one of the best farriers in the business, to Jack's mind, and might well have lost those teeth bent over the hind leg of a nervous or fly-bothered horse.

Stu never talked much, which suited Jack just fine. He had a way of listening, squinting his eyes up, nodding or grunting, that made him a real good audience. Hank asked Jack where he was off to, turning to look over his shoulder at Jack's dog and the duffel bag, but Stuart just rested both elbows on the table and leaned in closer so he could hear.

Jack hadn't prepared an answer to Hank's question, so he started in where he had left off the other night with Stu, complaining about the selling price of beef in the futures markets. After he'd ordered another round for their table, he mentioned to Hank that he was going on a little vacation—"Well, it's about time," Hank interjected quickly—to Las Vegas. Maybe he'd see a girlie show, Jack stated, winking over his raised mug, and lose his daughter's inheritance at the craps table.

Hank bought the next round, but Jack hardly noticed; he was going on about how his family had been ranching in this country since the early 1880's, holding out against drought and hard winters, calf-gutting lions and them damn, mangy elk. "Hell, I know I haven't gotten rich, but that ain't the point, is it? The thing is to keep the operation going, to keep ranching."

Except now there was a new enemy. "How in the hell does a man trying to feed his family fight the United States government? If that wormy little Cameron fellow doubles my grazing fees, he's going to put me right out of business. And then what? Hell, ninety percent of my land would be worth nothing without grazing. There's nothing else to do out here. And if the ranches are shut down, what's going to happen to this town—or Elgin or Safford? Who's gonna keep the Brown Barn afloat, am I right? Who's gonna shop at the grocery store, huh? Who's gonna hire the delinquents in the summers? You tell me.

"And how the hell do you even sell a ranch—if some poor fool wanted to—when the grazing fees are so high nobody but a millionaire could afford 'em? Who's goin' to pay me back for all them miles of fences I put in and all them stock tanks those god-damned elk are drinkin' out of every day?"

"I hear Cameron's goin' to be in Window Rock here one of these days," Hank offered when Jack stopped to gulp down the rest of his beer. "Trying to sell his rangeland reform stuff to the Indians maybe, huh?" That made Jack swallow wrong and he started choking, so Hank kept on. "It seems strange to me that a guy like Cameron is the one to do the ranchers in. Hell, his family's been in the business longer than yours, Jack."

Jack banged down his empty glass and stood up, weaving a little. He pointed a finger in Hank's face. "That ain't true," he said hotly, blinking to get his eyes straightened out. "We was here years afor them grocers showed up in Flagstaff. And I'm gonna stop right here afor I say more'n I mean to." He fumbled his wallet out of his back pocket and tossed some bills down on the table—probably not enough, but what the hell, he decided. He nodded gravely at Hank and said, "See ya' 'round, Stu," before he turned and left the table.

Jack had to pull out his wallet again to pay for the six-pack to go he ordered from Rusty, and Hud was standing up, waiting for him, when he reached the door. "Don't forget your bag, Jack," he heard Rusty call from behind the bar. Jack tapped the brim of his hat in a kind of salute and went back to grab his duffel bag. He pushed open the door and led Hud outside.

He had thought he'd stop by the Sonic for something to eat, but he had to pee really bad, so he headed straight out of town on the Interstate and got off at the first exit—87 North. He pulled onto the gravel edge of the highway and let Hud sniff around in the brush while he relieved himself. The night air was cool and the stars brilliant over the dark expanse of the Navajo Reservation. Jack didn't even need the wind this time to get the feeling he and Hud were riding high, but he did pop open one of the Budweisers when they climbed back in the truck and headed north.

Jack knew the territory south of I-40 intimately—much of it was his own land, after all. But in less than twenty minutes Jack had left the white world behind and entered the vast holdings of the Navajo Nation. The reservation was a foreign place to Jack; he knew they had their own laws and their own sense of the land, straddling the border between Arizona and New Mexico like the fifty states hadn't even been invented. And they ran mostly sheep or goats instead of cattle; wooly varmints that chewed pasture down to the dirt. The natives even had their own time zone; Jack realized he'd lost an hour in a second's worth of driving, lost a portion of his life he would never retrieve.

It was a lonely drive in the dark, with hardly any traffic and houses so wide-spaced and dimly lit he could barely make them out from the road. The trading post at Ganado was still over 60 miles away; Window Rock and his planned encounter with the Secretary of the Interior was another 40 miles beyond that. To pass the time, Jack started off telling Hud what he was going to say to the man once he had his full attention.

To Jack's mind, it was a war, a range war, East versus West, those arrogant environmentalists against hard-working businessmen like himself. "I remember how Dad used to say you had to *despise* your cows to run 'em on some of this land," he said, gesturing with yet another beer in his hand. "It ain't right and it ain't fair to charge us like they do the ranchers back east. What is it they want? Somethin' like eight bucks a head a month¾Jesus!"

Jack missed the first turnoff and had to take another road to back-track over to Dilkon, then all the way to Indian Wells he imagined the stand-off with the Tribal Police—well, and who knew who all else? The FBI? The Secret Service? Maybe shooting the man wasn't the thing. Maybe he'd take Cameron hostage, get him to sign something, a pledge not to put ranchers like him out of business. Then what? A sudden charge, his pistol blasting—get them to do the deed he had no stomach for.

Jack had to stop and pee again, but he waited until he knew he'd taken the right road to get to Ganado. Then he knew he was drunk when, instead of easing gently off onto the side of the road like he'd intended, the truck skidded to a stop in the gravel and nearly dropped off the steep embankment into the ditch. Hud slid right off the seat and landed with a clatter on top of the empty beer cans littering the floor.

He didn't have much farther to drive, Jack kept telling himself once they were back on the road—maybe another hour. He'd get some sleep after they'd made it to Window Rock. He'd just passed the little settlement that huddled around the Hubbell Trading Post, the houses a deeper black against the black night, and was cresting a low hill when the cows lounging in the middle of the warm road were lit up by his headlights.

Jack stood on the brake and Hud fell onto the beer cans again. "Shit!" Jack heard himself holler, then he swerved around the last cow, over-corrected, and sent the truck into a spin. A back wheel hit the gravel and the truck landed, driver's side down, in the ditch.

Jack lay there a minute, all out of breath, partly because the dog had climbed up onto his chest and lay there trembling with his nose resting right under Jack's ear. He had to climb out from under Hud to turn the engine off, then he poked his head out the open passenger's window. A few of the cows hadn't even stood up, but all of them had their heads turned and were musing stupidly over the wreck. "Fucking cattle," Jack fumed, straining to hoist himself up onto the door frame. "You bastards are going to be the death of me yet."

EIGHTEEN

My Great-Grandpa Jack's the one who started it all, and not just this obsession with a certain place whose dust you've inhaled so long it starts to form your own and your children's bones. He was the one who made them all believe he owned the land, that he could rule it.

I told Richard a little of his story over our first meal together. I hadn't really agreed to a date; I think I had just giggled into my empty coffee cup when he'd suggested we get together again sometime. But the very next Tuesday he'd showed up at the library, right at closing time. I almost told him he'd have to come back the next day, thinking he was there to check out a book, but when he saw I was ready to leave he just stepped back through the door and held it open for me. He was talking about restaurants, and I was still fumbling through my purse to find my car keys. When he opened the passenger's door of his car I finally figured out I was going with him.

He took me to Anderson's Steak House, which was a big mistake, but, of course, he couldn't have known that. And it's still one of the nicest restaurants in town, so I got the point. But all I could find on the menu to order was a salad, and the pieces of lettuce were so big I ended up just pushing them around on my plate instead of eating, and I still helped Richard drink a pitcher of beer. Maybe that's why I told him the great-grandfather story: too much beer and all those old ranching photographs the owner of the restaurant had hanging on the walls.

I had heard the edited version of the story from Alfredo; sometimes Dad would come home early from a night at the Brown Barn and while he drank his series of whiskey nightcaps he'd make me listen to his elaborate rendition of the ranch's glory days, invariably ending with the story of his Grandpa Jack's last stand. What I told Richard was a lot closer to the truth: my great-grandfather had been a foolish man who had gotten himself killed—leaving his wife and five sons to struggle on their own—because he'd believed he was indestructible. And he wasn't.

Richard had gotten Dad's spin on the story the next time I'd seen him, when he'd come to dinner at the ranch. That first date had ended with an awkward handshake—I remember how foolish I'd felt, standing in the library parking lot next to my car while he fumbled for my hand. I had just wanted to go, to get out of there, but he'd held onto my fingers. I think I invited him out to the ranch to put an end to it. To let Dad put an end to it.

But I had underestimated Richard. He'd weathered Dad's blustering with a smile—a smile! Poor *Tío* Fred had his head down almost to his mashed potatoes by the end of the meal, but Richard was sitting back in his chair with his fingers laced behind his neck. He'd lean forward to sip his coffee and nod at Dad, smiling all the while, like this fantastic story of a cowboy hero confronting a gang of lawless rustlers and single-handedly rescuing a prized bull was not the stuff of pulp fiction or even an inflated family legend but true.

After dinner Fred had made up some problem with one of the horses that he thought Dad would want to see to—at least, I think he made it up—to give Richard and me some time alone. I was grateful Dad was not there to see Richard clear the table. Then he'd wanted to help me with the dishes, and Richard had not only dried them, he'd actually found the proper place for each plate and glass in the cupboard, still smiling, because it wasn't Dad he was so pleased to be with; it was me.

I gave him a tour of the house after that. I showed him my desk in the storeroom, and we agreed that he would help me set up a real accounting system for the ranch. Richard hadn't been very interested in Dad's gun collection or his mounted barbed wire samples, but he spent quite a bit of time looking through the books I'd filled the rest of the living room shelves with. Then I took him upstairs, supposedly to show him the quilt Grandma Elizabeth had made. I was still sleeping in the front bedroom then, using the quilt as a bedspread, and I remember

Richard had admired it while standing in the threshold like he was afraid to follow me the rest of the way in.

I'd taken his hand to lead him into Dad's bedroom because I wanted to show him the garden from his window—this window; I was always so proud of the green riot spreading below. Richard's fingers had tightening their hold on mine—maybe he'd felt uneasy in another man's bedroom. But his other hand had found the small of my back by the time I'd finished pointing out the plants in each row. It was a mild summer evening like this one, and the garden had practically glowed. I remember offering to give him as many squash and tomatoes as he wanted, but he'd laughed and said, no, he didn't cook much, now that he was living alone.

Well, that's certainly changed—I can smell something wonderful wafting up the stairs from where he's busy in the kitchen. But at the time I remember Richard had given that embarrassed laugh again and pulled my hip against his as we stood just about here in what had been Dad's room; I got flustered and moved over to the other window to show him from this vantage point how you could see the ranch stretching out . . . .

But wait—this is wrong. I am jolted from reverie into a nightmare: the sky's orange, and there's an acrid smell of smoke, and then I see the flames—oh, my God, oh, my God—climbing over the roof of Dad's trailer.

I drop the nightgown I had been intending to pack for the trip to the hospital and struggle to open the window. Alfredo's down there, a small black shape spot-lighted by the shifting light of the fire, holding a garden hose. I need to open the window so I can scream to him, can scream for my father, but I give up and lurch around the bed to the door.

Richard catches me at the top of the stairs. He's out of breath, a dish towel still draped over one shoulder, panicked but trying to calm *me* down: "I called the fire department, Kate. They're on their way. Settle down, now. It's okay. He's not here. At least, I think he's gone. The truck's gone."

But I still push my way down the stairs to the porch and the noxious smell that had been seeping through the windows hits me like a blow to the gut. I'm gagging on it, but I keep stumbling toward it, into the haze. There's Alfredo, wide-eyed, waving me back, but I rush forward like an idiot, like I'm going to embrace the fireball consuming the little trailer. It's the heat that forces me away, and then Richard is helping me up off the ground. I'm having another contraction, so I let him hold me while I sob and sob, then I can't help it—I start to laugh: Alfredo looks so comical, squirting that puny stream of water from the hose that evaporates before it hits the ground. All three of us end up watching from the porch, streaks of black, like war paint, on our stricken faces, on our clothes.

NINETEEN

I took Tristan to save him—well, at least the first time. Frank was anything but subtle, and I lived in the same damn house, after all, so I knew what was going on better than Guy did. I mean, I can kind of see why Guy didn't get it at first because, for a while, Frank really did seem to be going along with Lily's dream of creating a big, fancy Arabian show horse operation, and he certainly bankrolled all those improvements the bitch and Guy dreamed up after the fire took out the old stable. But the sicker Frank got the more he seemed to worry about money—or worrying about all the money he was spending was making Frank sicker. Who the fuck knows? I'm sure me being a mopey little asshole who threw tantrums every other day didn't help much, either. And even stupid Frank must have known *something* was going on between those two. Anyway it wasn't long before Frank was making phone calls he didn't want Lily—or anyone else, for that matter—to hear. He told the people on the other end of the line stuff like he was "in over his head," that he was "over extended." No f-ing kidding—those horses cost a fortune

Sometimes I think it was his sister he was talking to. I was usually outside in the flower bed under his half-opened window, and I could just make out her witchy screeching—she hated Lily and what she called her "dreams of glory." But this time Frank wasn't begging for another handout of family money. This time he was talking to someone with a slow, deep voice, and Frank was going on and on about what prize-winners our horses were, or would be, and when a man showed up the next day I didn't wait to find out which horse he had come for. I took Tristan to get him the hell away from there, to keep him. I couldn't imagine a life without that horse, I loved him so f-ing much. I still can't.

This was the first time I took him, after I'd gotten kicked out of that boarding school near Prescott. I hadn't even really ridden Tristan before, just "backed" him that one time with Guy holding his reins, so he was still really green, and the wind was blowing, making the horses stamp around in their stalls, but I didn't think about all that stuff. I snatched a bridle and a saddle, threw open the stall door, cinched him up as quick as I could, grabbed a handful of mane, and launched us both into a f-ing freak out of a dust storm, racing him down the lane toward the canal road. Man, that f-ing horse could run! But he wasn't trained, and once I got him going I couldn't stop him, and I got scared, and I think that spooked him even more because the next thing I knew I was spitting dirt out of my mouth and staring at the toe of Guy's boot.

He carried me all the way back—that's how I know he used to love me. He told me the horse was safe so I'd stop crying, and then he didn't listen to Lily shouting at him that I was just pretending to be hurt to get out of the mound of shit I was in. The problem was Lily was right—I'd twisted my ankle in the fall and it did hurt a little, but I was really okay and mostly just wanted Guy to pay attention to *me* instead of *her* for a change. And I wanted to tell him what Frank was up to. I thought Guy would understand why I'd run off on his horse once I'd told him. But then Guy got so mad at me and I wouldn't do it. So it didn't stop there. Frank didn't stop trying to sell Tristan until Guy killed him.

And I didn't stop stealing Tristan even then.

TWENTY

The boys were so excited that they set out at once, tripping in the dark over the rocks and branches in their path, clanging to one knee and then groaning to heft themselves back to their feet in their heavy armor. They walked all night, heading east to where their father had promised to meet them and show them the rest of the way to the Big Giant's hideout.

White Shell Woman's son greeted the dawn with a huge yawn; Changing Woman's son removed his helmet and scratched his weary head. But they had made it. They stood at the very edge of the world where the earth and sky meet.

Soon the light grew strong enough to make out the landscape around them, and as they watched a ray sliced through the low clouds to illuminate a distant peak: *Tsoodzil*, the Blue Bead Mountain. "There," Changing Woman's son exclaimed. "That must be where we'll find Big Giant." He replaced his helmet and smacked it down tight. White Shell Woman's son raised his blade, turning it to catch the light.

The warriors were eager but untested. They knew their enemy well enough to fear him, a giant so huge his shadow marked the distance a man could travel on a day-long march. And they still had far to go on the little food their father had been able to provide them and no sleep. But they pressed on, now dragging the heavy quiver of arrows, or shrugging sore shoulders under their armor, or wiping away the sweat that dripped constantly out from under their helmets.

At the base of Blue Bead Mountain they found *Tósido*, Warm Spring, and they dropped to their knees to drink from its deep blue waters. For a moment the warriors were boys again, splashing each other playfully. Then they heard it, felt it: the thunderous pulse of a giant's footsteps, coming closer.

TWENTY-ONE

Hud had almost stopped shaking by the time Jack decided not to wait by the side of the highway any longer. Even if there had been any traffic out in the middle of the reservation at this time of night, it wasn't a ride he needed—he needed a big truck with a winch or maybe a tractor that could get him back on the road.

So instead of walking a few miles back to the trading post at Ganado, Jack picked up his duffel bag and crossed the highway to check out the dirt track that wandered north, into the blackness of the mesas. He stared hard at the dirt, rubbing his sore shoulder. Big tire prints—there must be a ranch or a farm or two up this way.

Hud stayed right at Jack's heels until they scared up a rabbit, and then the dog took off after it, leaving Jack to stumble alone over the ruts in the road. There was a sliver of a moon now, but it was still too dark for Jack to see more than a few feet ahead. He did know he was walking up a slow grade from how hard he was breathing, and he could see where the stars were blacked out by a low cliff to the west. He was about to whistle the dog back and turn around when he saw the boxy shape of a building against the eastern horizon. He left the road to inspect it.

There were no lights and it was too small to be a house, but Jack nursed the hope that it was an out-building of some kind, which would mean there'd be an inhabited dwelling somewhere nearby. But as he stumbled closer, Jack saw the walls were in disrepair, fallen in on themselves, and when he got close enough to touch it he recognized the fitted stones and mud mortar of an Anasazi ruin.

"Shit," he wheezed. There were ruins just like this one all along the flood plain of the Little Colorado River and down almost every one of its tributaries, including the washes that ran through Jack's ranch. Jack's dad had told him there had probably been more people living on their land and in the surrounding countryside in the 1100's than there were now—the stone walls of former cities littered the mesa tops of Jack's Canyon and Chavez Pass. In fact, in some places the mounds of what had been several story buildings humped the ground for a half-mile around, and pottery shards crunched underfoot no matter where you tried to walk.

Jack Senior had taken quite a bit of interest in the thick, rock walls and outlines of dirt-filled rooms. He'd leave the hard work of rounding up strays to Jack and the rest of the outfit and wander off by himself to "the fort," as they called it, a series of low walls on a high promontory that overlooked the creek hundreds of feet below.

Come lunch time, Jack or Fred would be sent to retrieve him, and when Jack rode up he'd find Jack Senior's horse ground-tied and his father nearby, using his boot to toe through the rubble of rocks, all the while scratching at his beard, deep in thought, or sitting in the shade with his back against one of the low walls. One time, when Jack had dismounted and walked over to give the older man a hand up, his father had asked him, "Why do ya suppose there's so many lizards around these places?" like he really wanted to know—and like Jack could've answered a question like that.

Right now Jack felt like kicking the rest of the old wall down, he was that tired and discouraged. He put his fingers in his mouth and whistled shrilly for Hud, backing up a few steps to peer over the dark mesa for the dog.

The next instant Jack was falling. His feet dropped right out from under him and his duffel bag was wrenched up over his head. He scraped the length of his back and jammed one leg hard against the ground as he landed. Then sticks and dirt were raining down on top of him. Jack rolled onto his side and covered his head. A moment later he was sitting up, howling.

The shape of Hud's head, his ears cocked, filled the opening above him. Jack would have strangled the mutt with his bare hands if he could have reached him. "God damn it to hell," Jack roared, the arch of pain shooting up his leg and into his back. Jack was panting with it, lifting himself up off the ground with his hands, trying to straighten out the leg, to lean away from it.

The pit echoed with his own noise and Jack covered his ears and gritted his teeth but still the guttural moans kept coming until his throat was sore and his jaw ached. He was covered with sweat, shivering, still panting, but he had to stop this, he had to pull himself together.

Jack had been thrown from a horse and rolled on, so he knew he could survive a measly broken leg. He'd had a bad wreck in a truck the week after he'd gotten his discharge from the army and he'd recovered from those injuries in record time. And his right collarbone; that had been shattered against the bunk house wall when Ed Ruffner had gone crazy after guzzling a jug of bad whiskey. His nose, too, had been broken in a fight, that time at the Brown Barn right after Lucy died. He'd weather this.

Hud was whining and scratching at the roof of mud and wooden beams over his head while Jack worked desperately to calm himself. The clumps of dirt falling on and around him started Jack hyperventilating again—those other times there had been people around. Why, at the Brown Barn, Tom—or had it been Oren—had been right there to offer him a hand up. He'd hustled Jack out the saloon door and into the truck.

"Help!" Jack shouted. "Help! Help me! God-damn it, help!"

But only Hud responded, digging furiously until he managed to dislodge one of the beams. It dropped into the pit with a dull thud, narrowly missing Jack, and a small section of the roof collapsed around it. Jack started screaming again: "Stop it! Stop! Get away!" Hud had scrambled backwards to avoid falling in and now he poked his head tenuously into the hole—a black shape blotting out the star-studded sky beyond. The dog looked down at Jack and whimpered. "Git!" Jack shouted, and the dog's head disappeared.

Jack wiped his face with his hands; the sweat made the dirt cling to him, there was dirt in his hair, his eyes, his mouth. Think, he told himself. You are in a hole somebody dug, in a trap for large game of some kind. The hunter will come along any minute to see what kind of trophy he's got for his den. But he knew it wasn't just a hole.

Jack dragged himself on his butt until he felt the wall at his back. No, not the wall, a bench, he realized, pulling himself up, gasping with the effort, a low bench that followed the curve of a carefully constructed stone wall. Okay, a *kiva* then. He'd fallen backwards like an idiot into an abandoned *kiva*.

Jack sneezed from the dust and cried out again. Hud put both paws and his whole head down the hole this time, and Jack knew he was thinking about jumping in. "Git!" Jack yelled at him. "Don't be a god-damned fool."

How do people get out of *kivas*, Jack asked himself. His dad would have known; in fact, his dad had probably told him. Jack groaned. His teeth were chattering now; he was still sweating, still panting. The old man would have mentioned it in the middle of a bunch of other boring facts and speculations, or he'd have passed it along as something his friend—what was that guy's name, the druggist—had told him. That old pot-hunter had robbed graves all over the territory. Jack Senior would lean against the counter at the pharmacy for hours, listening to his friend's adventures, turning over in his hands whatever the other man had found.

When the noise of his own breathing quieted Jack heard a scurrying sound—there it was again. And what was that? A sound like a sigh. Jack held perfectly still and listened. Maybe it was just the dirt sifting down from the roof where the dog still waited. Jack patted his empty shirt pocket, then shifted his weight, sending a shock of pain up his leg, to feel in his pants pockets for matches. Of course, he wasn't carrying any. He wished to hell he smoked and it was lung cancer that was eating him alive right then.

Then he remembered his duffel bag. He knew he hadn't packed any matches, but the pistol—the pistol—was in there. Jack lowered himself carefully back down onto the floor, biting his lower lip, and felt around cautiously. He was so jumpy he called out in surprise when he touched the end of the wooden beam. But it wasn't just a beam—there was a cross bar. A wooden ladder.

Jack's laugh rang strangely in his ears. He struggled to lift the ladder but he had no leverage and the exertion left him panting again. Jack scooted backwards over the dirt floor, hurrying now, ignoring his throbbing leg. He dragged the ladder with him to the bench. Then he rested, his heart pounding, but still his arms gave out when he tried to pull himself back up on the bench and he had to wait a little longer before he could heave himself and the ladder onto the low ridge of stones along the wall.

The ladder's legs were uneven; one beam was rotted to a splintered stump just below the last rail. Jack couldn't see the other end where it rested in the dirt, but he decided to make it the base. He put all his weight on his own good leg and stood up, bracing himself with a hand against the wall. Then he slowly raised the ladder and used it like a crutch to hobble under the hole in the roof.

He was weaving, exhausted, but somehow the spokes of the ladder were now leaning against the roof beams, and Jack could see the stars and that narrow slice of a moon overhead. Hud yipped at him once and Jack could hear him pacing around.

Jack took a deep breath, testing the ladder where it rested against the beam. He still had to drag himself up it, and it looked to be damn near impossible.

Jack placed his hands on the highest crossbeam he could reach and hung there for a second while his foot found the lowest step, but as soon as he put his weight on the rail it split and Jack was dangling from his hands. He lowered himself carefully and paused to wipe his wet face and pull at his nose with one hand. Then he tried again, reaching up with both hands and putting his weight on the second step, but the wood was ancient, rotted, and the rail cracked under his boot. "God damn it," Jack howled in frustration. But he was determined; once again he grabbed the crossbeam over his head and strained to pull himself up.

When he reached with one hand for the next rail, one of the legs split length-wise and Jack lost his balance. He landed on his butt with a woof of expelled air and the ladder dropped in two pieces, one on top of and one beside him. Jack didn't even push the splintered wood off his chest. He didn't move.

TWENTY-TWO

By the time the fire truck wailed in from the highway the trailer was just a smoldering pile of charcoal. I allowed Richard to coax me back into the house, and I talked to the fire chief and then the sheriff while lying under the huge hump of my stomach on the couch. The contractions were still maybe twenty minutes apart, and I told each of them that I was not budging until somebody found my father, even though Richard had finished packing my overnight bag and had already put it in the car.

I asked them to check the Brown Barn first, and when the sheriff came back from the phone he said I'd been right, Jack had been there—with Hud, no less. Then Richard told them about Dad's medical condition and the men took their discussion into the kitchen. I couldn't hear their words but they were debating something in ominous tones. I knew Dad was down in the dumps about his illness and acting even more cantankerous than usual, but what would purposefully torching the trailer accomplish? It had to have been a mistake; a faulty wire in a lamp, maybe—*Tio* Fred had said he'd seen a light on. But when the men came tromping back into the living room they went straight to the gun case on the wall, wanting to assess its contents, and I had to haul myself up, complaining that the damn thing had been locked for months, and work the combination on the bicycle lock I'd put on there after Dad had threatened that poor Game and Fish guy. They could see the rifles and Grandma's old pump-action shotgun in their slots, dusty as hell, I realized. I left the lock off and went to grab a rag to wipe Dad's treasures clean. It seemed important, at the time.

Then it took another hour for the sheriff and Richard to finish their chin-scratching and speculating on the porch. I was back on the couch, with a pad of paper, and a pencil, now, noting the time that each contraction started, and watching them through the screen door. Once the firemen had thoroughly doused the smoldering ashes they rumbled their truck back down the drive and things got quiet enough to hear that the horses were still raising hell, whinnying and snorting. Finally I heard the sheriff's car door slam and the gravel pop as he wheeled past the house. It scared me, for some reason. I'd spent my whole life on this wide swath of lonesome and never felt this brand of afraid before. But tonight the place had an emptiness to it that was entirely new.

Richard tip-toed in and took a look at my contractions chart. "Do you want to head into town?" he whispered—even though there was just the two of us in the house.

"No," I pouted. I folded my arms across my big, new boobs and tried to make it clear that I was planted there until Dad came slinking home. Then I was dozing on and off, waking long enough to note the time on the mantel clock at the start of each contraction. Around 4 a.m. the house had settled into a deep quiet and I could finally cry in peace for my father. Richard had fallen asleep in the Lay-Z-Boy next to me, so I whimpered as quietly as I could.

But it was Hud I woke up thinking about. This dark-haired girl looking down on me from the foot of the couch would never have been able to enter my home unannounced if Hud had been here where he belonged. Richard snorted awake when he heard me pleading with her: "Where is he? Tell me. Where is my father?"

TWENTY-THREE

I don't believe I'm really all that dangerous. I don't hear voices in my head, telling me to do creepy shit. Whenever I've done creepy shit it's because I felt like doing it. *I'm* in charge of me—no one, no *thing* else. I realize that makes some of the things I've done worse, because I *did* know what the fuck I was doing.

But I'm better these days. I haven't even thought about launching a fit since I've been here. Could be it's the new meds, 'though if I'm all doped up on bi-polar shit and anti-depressants and still planning my end game—I don't know. Most likely I act more like a "normal" teenager—whatever the fuck *that* means—because of the lack of what Dr. Maynard used to call my "trigger events," which was code for Lily, mostly, but also any kind of authority lording their wise asses over me, telling me what to do, and generally pissing me off. He said it went back to stuff that must've happened to me when I was younger, maybe when I was too young to even remember. That's a little disturbing, you know? That bad stuff could've happened that you don't even f-ing remember, and you're still reeling from it? Talk about creepy shit.

I do remember spending a lot of time locked away somewhere, in a closet, then the bathroom after I peed in Lily's shoes and made her mad, in a bedroom once she got Frank to marry her. I'd read, mostly, or write in my journal. Then at some point I'd try the door and it'd be open again. Right away I'd sneak out to mess around with the horses or spy on Guy and Lily.

Anyway, now that I'm on my own I'm not as angry as I was before. Sometimes I'd just shake with it, a boiling rage, a compulsion to stab a pillow to death or rip something up. My hands became claws, my teeth became fangs, my voice a roar. The worst I get now is a little huffy if some kid takes the seat I always sit in on the bus. I might have grabbed that kid by the hair before. Now I just sit behind him and keep crossing and uncrossing my legs, knocking my knees against the back of his seat until I've made his kidneys sore—or at least I hope they're sore by the time we get to school.

I'm better in class, now, too. Still ADHD, of course, but they take that into consideration here at this school, so it's okay to get up and sharpen your pencil about a zillion times a day. I tested well enough to enroll as a junior here. I'm good at math, once I sit down to it, and even better in English class if I take the time to actually read the book, and even with all the school I've missed over the years I'll start my senior year in the fall—that is if I change my mind and decide not to off myself, but I don't know why I'd do *that*. So if you're reading this, after I'm gone, here's the point: being crazy doesn't mean you're stupid. I don't want people writing me off as a dumb ass after I'm gone.

Social studies is my new favorite, and I like going to the after school program, too, all because of Mr. C. He reminds me of Guy some, in that he talks to us like we're regular people instead of a bunch of fuck ups. He actually tries to get us to care about what's going on in the environment and the history of our country and human rights and crap like that. While the other kids snicker and joke around I try to take his questions seriously, and he listens to my answers, maybe even moving his glasses closer to his eyes like he's trying to see better where I'm coming from. He's a bit of a hippie throw back, I think, judging from what he says about the government. His hair's longer than the other teachers' too.

That's why I was almost actually excited when Paula told me I'd be going out there—I actually felt this wave of happy. Mr. C. lives on an old ranch way outside of town, and they need me to work my stable girl wonders out there for a while. I'm up for it. It's pretty damn boring around the home here in the summer time. And, like I said, I like Mr. C., and I really don't think I'm dangerous. Except to myself, of course. No one else has to worry about me. I don't *think*.

TWENTY-FOUR

Boom! Boom! Boom! Like thunder bouncing off canyon walls, the Big Giant's footsteps put fear into the hearts of the waiting boys. They scrambled behind a bolder and pulled branches over their heads but they were peeking through the leaves as he approached, too fascinated by his hairy hugeness to look away as he came into view, carrying a net full of bloody prey. As they watched he dropped to all fours and drank deeply from the spring.

He slurped up the water, paused to burp so loudly it hurt their ears, then bent to drink again. Only once he had drained the spring down to its bubbling source did the giant sit back and wipe his face with the back of one hand. "There!" his voice boomed, "I drank it all! Good for me!"

Of course it was not good for the boys or all the other animals now cowering in the brush. Changing Woman's son felt his terror at the sight of the monster shifting to anger. This giant must be stopped, and he and White Shell Woman's son were the only ones with even the slightest chance of doing so. He heard his companion gasp as he stood up. He fitted a lightning arrow into his bow and said, "Your days of drinking and feasting are over, Big Giant. We have come to slay you!" He looked down at White Shell Woman's son so he would stand tall beside him, and the other boy rose from his crouch. He also took an arrow from his sheath and pulled his bowstring taunt.

But the giant only laughed and stomped his feet, making the rocks around them jump. "You tiny things could never hurt *me*," he roared. "But you do look delicious!"

Changing Woman's son loosed his arrow; it plunged deep into the giant's chest, and the noise of the giant's pain and surprise nearly knocked the boy over backwards. Then White Shell Woman's son fired his arrow into one of the monster's eyes, and as the giant screamed again and pulled the arrow out, all of his brains flowed out after it. He tottered for a moment; it was not clear which way he'd fall. Then he dropped face forward, landing only inches from their feet. The earth shook and the dust sent White Shell Woman's son into a coughing fit.

TWENTY-FIVE

Something crawled into the palm of Jack's upturned hand and he woke up gasping, flicking his wrist to dislodge it. He was almost to his feet before he remembered his broken leg and he had to sag down, with his forehead almost touching the dirt, and wait for the wave of pain to pass.

It was morning; Jack could see the shape of the *kiva* when he raised his head. He looked over his shoulder to where a beam of light illuminated the motes of dust in the air to the west of the entrance hole.

There was his duffel bag. Jack wondered how he had avoided tripping over it in the dark. He tossed the pieces of the ladder out of his way and pulled himself toward it, stretched to grab its strap with his fingers, then rolled up to a sitting position with the bag on his lap. He had fumbled open one of his medicine bottles and tossed two pain pills in his mouth before he realized his throat was parched and he had no water to wash them down with. For several minutes he moaned and gagged and concentrated on swallowing.

"Now what?" Jack asked himself, then he was sorry he had spoken out loud. He saw right away where the answering sound had come from, and he inched away from it on his butt until his back was against the bench again. He put one arm on the stones to pull himself up but he couldn't turn his head away from it.

The snake was uncoiling itself, its head up and circling, tongue flicking in and out. It looked at Jack with yellow eyes. A big snake—too big to be a rattler, Jack reassured himself, but his heart was pounding and his arms shivered under the weight of his body as he struggled back onto the bench. He leaned down, wincing, grabbed his duffel bag and straightened his broken left leg. Just a bull snake, grown long and fat from feasting on deer mice and desert rats.

Jack opened the bag and took the pistol out, debating whether to kill it. He wondered how long the snake had been down in this hole and if it wanted out—or maybe it could slither in and out. Hud must have heard him moving around because the dog had his head down in the hole again and was sniffing noisily. "Should I shoot it?" Jack asked the dog, and then he did, or tried to. He missed the first time and the report was so loud inside the *kiva* that Jack cringed and cupped a hand over his ear; he noted the dog scrambling off. But then he aimed again, holding his breath this time, and blasted the snake's head off.

The next three shots Jack fired at the blue sky showing through the entrance hole. He almost emptied the chamber, thinking this was his best chance of attracting someone's attention. But he decided with his finger still on the trigger that the last bullet might be needed for something else.

Jack cupped the pistol in his lap all morning, waiting to be rescued. He was already hot, thirstier than he'd ever been, hungry, but the pills had dulled the pain in his bowels and leg, so he dozed, hunched over on the bench, dreaming that he was walking along the bottom of the ocean and he could breathe the thick, warm, salty water.

TWENTY-SIX

The girl was about to answer me. I watched her mouth begin to form the words, but then there was a stout woman coming up behind her saying, "Oh, I'm so sorry, Kate—I hope she didn't wake you. Jane, sweetheart, did you even knock?" A Navajo woman in a print dress, clutching a briefcase—at least *she* looked familiar. And then Richard was standing up, smearing some of the soot on his face around as he tried to rub away sleep.

"Who are you?" I asked, up on my elbows, now. My big belly seemed ready to sink me into the couch. "What do you want?"

"It's okay, Kate. This is Jane, and you've met Paula before," Richard gestured at the women. "I'm sorry—we've had . . . . It was a rough night."

"Oh, yes," Paula exclaimed. "We saw there was a fire. Was it a trailer? No one was hurt, I hope."

"No—well, no. Here, let me get some coffee started." Richard was ushering Paula toward the kitchen, but the girl was more interested in me, I guess. Another contraction had me panting, my hands gripping the sides of my stomach as if it was trying to go somewhere without me.

"You're having a baby," the girl stated.

I groaned to sit up as the contraction eased, then stretched for the pencil and pad of paper on the coffee table. I checked the mantel clock; still eighteen minutes apart.

"Aren't you supposed to go to a hospital when you're having a baby?" she asked. She had settled onto the bolstered arm of the couch. In her teens, very pale, wearing a black T-shirt and jeans, black tennis shoes. She'd be pretty if she'd brush her hair, I decided—her eyes were a striking blue under those too-long bangs.

I only shook my head in response. I was determined to be right on that couch when Jack got back from whatever misadventure he'd wandered off on now. I wanted to give him hell about the trailer, make him feel bad for worrying me so. But first there was work to do—that *someone* had to do: "I've got a corral full of horses and a stallion in the barn," I told the girl. "They need to be fed and have their water troughs filled. Our stableman, Fred, is too banged up to take care of them."

Richard was calling from the kitchen, "Jane? Jane, can you come in here for a second?"

But the girl didn't seem to hear him. "I'm cool with that," she told me.

I lay back on the couch, regarding her. I knew the kid wasn't deaf. "What's your real name?" I asked.

That made the girl stand up and start for the kitchen.

"Wait just a minute," I said. "I asked you a question." The girl turned back to me, her eyes in narrow slits now. "Just a minute," I said more loudly so Richard would hear me. "Things can happen around horses—that's how Fred got hurt. If someone needs to shout a warning, it helps to have the right name. I wouldn't want nothin' to happen to you, hon."

Richard was in the hallway. "You okay, Kate?"

I nodded. "I'm okay. Been better." I interlaced my fingers over my belly, keeping my eyes on the girl. What she decided to do next would make up my mind about her. She might be done after a morning feed run.

"I'm just going to take Jane down to meet Fred and get her set up. You're staying here for awhile, okay, kiddo? Right, Kate? She can have Jack's old room."

"What about Dad?" I asked him. He seemed to have forgotten—or given up . . . .

"He'll have to decide that. He can stay with Fred in the bunk house, or we'll fix up the downstairs bedroom." Richard gave me the look that meant we'd talk about it later. He turned back to the girl: "You guys will be holdin' down the fort while Kate and I are at the hospital."

"I'm waitin' for Dad," I said, turning my attention to the ceiling, "right here." But I didn't sound nearly as convincing as I meant to be. I glanced over at Richard, by the screen door, now, motioning for the girl to follow him.

"Rose," the girl said to me in a whisper. Then she turned and trailed out after him.

TWENTY-SEVEN

"Jane Doe" was the name the cops in Flagstaff wrote at the top of their form; I kind of liked that—not being Rose anymore, the horse murderer. So I kept saying that's what people should call me, even after they transferred me over to Winslow with my real name on the papers they handed over to Paula. She said it was okay. She said sometimes it's important to make a fresh start, and a new name can be a part of that. She must have actually read that report they gave her about all the crap good ol' Rose had pulled—the messed up runaway. And maybe it's helped. The only trouble Jane's been in so far has been for disobeying the lights out rule by staying up late writing in this journal under the covers.

Now I'm not even breaking that rule—I'm sitting right here at a kitchen table, a kitchen table in the middle of a sunny kitchen in the middle of the day.

God, I haven't even thought about suicide since I got here. I wouldn't have now if I hadn't written about doing it on nearly every one of these pages. Suddenly I can't even remember why killing myself has seemed so f-ing important. When I saw that stallion today, I swear to God, I just went crazy with something, I don't know—relief?

I know it's not the same horse—I'm not stupid. I mean, I know in my head that it couldn't be. He's a whole hand taller, thicker in his haunches, but he looks so much like a little bit older Tristan would, without the Arabian arch in his neck. He's pure black like Tristan was, with those big-lashed, smart, brown eyes. It was creepy but *good* creepy, almost like magic. I took one look at him and that weight, that feeling like I'm suffocating, lifted. I don't even think I *knew* I felt that way until it stopped. Then I could have floated right off the f-ing planet; I think I almost did.

The others are gone now: Paula, Mr. C. and his wife, gone back to Winslow. They left me with the old Mexican guy, Fred, a bunch of cattle horses, and that black stallion. His name is Midnight.

It's amazing, really, how trusting some people can be.

TWENTY-EIGHT

Changing Woman's son hurried over to the fallen giant and toed his huge hand. Nothing happened. He walked all the way around him, a circuit that took several minutes, stopping to prod or kick the monster along the way. When he got to the giant's shaggy head, White Shell Woman's son was already there with his knife out, hacking away at the giant's scalp. "Whoa, look at you," Changing Woman's son called to his friend. "I've got a good name for you. You should be called *Na'ídígishí*, 'He Who Cuts the Life Out of the Enemy.'"

"*Na'ídígishí*," White Shell Woman's son repeated as he straightened from his work. "I like that! So then," he said, remembering the bravery his friend had shown when he had stood tall and challenged the giant, "I have a name for you, as well. You should be called *Naayéé' neizghání*! For you are indeed a Monster Slayer, that much is clear."

He Who Cuts the Life Out of the Enemy and Monster Slayer grinned at one another over the fallen mountain of their enemy. They knew they had shown themselves to be brave and strong. They knew there would be songs about this victory. And they finally knew who they really were: worthy sons. It was time to return home with their prize.

TWENTY-NINE

The first thing Jack gave up on was the idea of hurting anybody, especially the Secretary of the Interior, no matter what the son-of-a-bitch did. The minute he got out of this hole, Jack was going to get his truck back on the road and head straight home—and he was going to drive slowly and carefully.

The booze was easy to swear off; he had a hangover, and at the moment he was sure liquor would never tempt him again. He even vowed to start taking his medicines like he was supposed to, and to demonstrate his good intentions, Jack took all of his pill bottles out of his duffel and lined them up on the bench beside him. But his mouth was bone dry, and the only ones he actually worked at swallowing were the pain pills, until he'd lost track of how many of those he'd forced down.

Hud had waited right at the edge of the pit in the full sun all morning, then he must have found some shade to lie in because he'd be absent for minutes at a time before returning to check on Jack, his tongue lolling half out of his head. Jack would yell something at the dog every time, call him a gloating idiot, a sad excuse for a dog, a worthless mutt.

When the sun was burning down near the center of the *kiva* the dog cast his shadow in on him again. Jack looked up and was blinded; he looked down and saw drops of moisture darkening the dirt. Hud shook himself and a fine spray of water rained down; the son-of-a-bitch had found a stock pond somewhere. Jack cursed the beast then until he ran out of wind.

At first Jack thought the *kiva* was infested with mice, but after a while he realized most of the scurrying sounds he was hearing were made by lizards. There were a lot of the garden-variety he saw every day on the steps of his trailer or clinging to the wall under the porch light at night, but also a fluorescent green, collared lizard like Jack had seen on the rock outcrops near Chavez Pass. A couple of horned toads mated, oblivious to Jack's misery, in the circle of sunlight on the floor. He railed at them, too, telling them he was god-damned company and they should have learned better manners than that.

He chewed down another bitter pain pill and stood up unsteadily, then he cupped both hands around his mouth and yelled for help again until he was hoarse and his throat burned. When Jack slumped back down on the bench his shoulders were shaking but he was too dry to make tears.

It was Richard his mind seized on then. What would Richard think if he could see him now? Jack straightened his sore back and sucked in his paunch. What would Richard do if he was the one stuck down here? "He'd be scratching poems in the dirt, what do you want to bet?" Jack said to the invisible dog. "Why he'd be inspired, he'd be in god-damned poet heaven." The metaphors were only too obvious, even to Jack—buried alive in this ancient ceremonial place. Jack stopped talking to pat his empty stomach, wondering how long it would take for his bones to start showing through his skin.

But wouldn't Richard be the one the others sent looking for him? Kate was in no shape to do it, and neither, now, was Fred, with that busted arm. Jack closed his eyes and imagined his son-in-law's goofy face, fringed with the black wavy hair of a clown, hanging upside-down through the entrance hole.

He had never told the girl the real reason he'd moved out of the house and into his trailer. Sure, it was to give them their own place and to stay clear of all the politics that go with a marriage, but there was a lot more to it. For one thing—and this was the part he could have told her, maybe should have told her, at the time—he wanted them to be happy there, on the ranch. He wanted—needed—her family to stay.

The other thing was personal, not really fitting for his daughter to hear. It had happened the day after Katie and Richard had returned from their honeymoon. Jack had stepped into the upstairs' shower and seen the other man's thick, black body hairs curling against the white porcelain and clogging up the drain. He'd had to touch the hairs to clear them out and it had made him gag.

Jack's people had a bit of German in their background but they were mostly of English and Irish bloodlines, and those traits won out. All the exposed parts of their fair skin burned under the sun into freckled leather, and the men had thin beards or went clean-shaven, with just a fine, brown fur on their chests and privates. He couldn't stomach the thought of this gorilla snoring just down the hall from him, of having to smell his stink in the bathroom, of seeing him bleary-eyed just after waking. The man wasn't family. To live with him struck Jack as indecent.

And hadn't his people all been like that, too? Jack's father had kept the woman he would marry in a hotel for years, visiting her in secret until Jack's grandmother died because the older woman had simply refused to share her home. It was his mom who had admitted this to him: "Grandma Grace was pioneer stock, through and through. You'd a thought she was the only woman on the planet, way she acted," she'd told him more than once. "Self-reliant ain't the word for it—if you weren't of the clan then you weren't."

Maybe the rebel in Grandpa Jack's blood had been a little too strong and had come down through the lines undiluted because they were still separatists at the core, every one of them. But how else do you stand the isolation? How else could you survive—hell, welcome—the endless summer days with nothin' but a herd of cows for company, a horizon empty but for a heat-warped line of scrub juniper way in the distance, or the winters that were just as interminable, only blank white instead of green and brown, and crack-your-teeth cold to boot. You had to love the sky blue and big as God because that was the most of it, every live-long day.

Jack waved away the flies and shifted his weight on the hard stone bench; his butt was sore from sitting for so long and even with all the pills he'd taken his leg throbbed unceasingly. He peered up at the piece of blue he could see through the roof until the dog's thick head appeared again. "Get me out of here, will you, Hud?" Jack asked the dog, using a civil tone for the first time since he'd landed. The dog wagged his whole torso and laid down with his front paws dangling over the edge. "We got to think of somethin'. A fella could die of thirst in here," Jack informed him, feeling his cracked lips with his fingers.

But his death still didn't seem possible, not really. Yeah, this cancer stuff had thrown him for a loop, all right, but there was something about being in this hole in this god-forsaken place that kind of put all that in perspective. Maybe he wouldn't get found until there was a corpse that stunk bad enough for someone to catch a whiff from the road. "Good thing I plugged that snake," he told Hud, laughing hoarsely. One thing Jack *didn't* want to be was a meal for a reptile.

Jack watched the dog scramble up and heard him moving off to find the shade again. "Hey, where ya going?" he called out after him. "You used to like suntannin' that black hide of yours, years ago."

There had been a time, right after Lucy died, when Jack had been troubled by thoughts of his own mortality, but he knew then to get up from the company around the campfire, select a fresh horse out of the remuda, tap his hat back into the permanent dent in his hair, wet his bandanna from whatever water was left in his canteen, and head out again, riding in circles around the musical lowing of a sleeping herd, pushing himself past tired all the way to exhaustion so later that night on his bedroll he could drop thoughtlessly into sleep and wake up to bird calls before dawn to start all over again.

And if he was home all he'd had to do was chase his three-year-old daughter down—he'd never seen a kid so good at hiding out, huddling on the floor of her closet while he went through the house hollering her name, or hunkering down under one of the bushes out back by the garden—and the morbid mood would leave him. It wasn't anything that Katie did, exactly. It was more how self-absorbed she was, saying no, no matter what she was asked, pouting, uncooperative; she never gave a thought to his suffering and, in her presence, neither did he.

"She's come to look a lot like her ma," he said out loud. Katie had her mother's slender frame and her same pretty face, the eyes that shaded from brown to green, depending on the weather, a narrow jaw and a mouth that turned down at the sides when she was relaxed.

Jack had studied that face quite a bit over the years, usually while the girl was watching something on television and he sat on the couch with the newspaper up in front of him like a shield. He'd worry about what was bothering her now, why her face was so sad, then she'd bust out laughing at a T.V. joke and he'd realize again that her expression had nothing to do with what she was feeling inside.

Lucy had been like that, too. Her face would be calm and she'd be silent as a rock when the storm of words raged at their fiercest inside. He would have to ask her questions, prod her into saying what had made her so mad.

And if he was mad, himself, he wouldn't do it. Let her stew in her own juices, he'd think—why did he have to ask for the abuse every time? After Katie was born he'd given it up and just let her be, and he had let himself revert to the loner he'd been when he met her.

Jack still couldn't help a smile, thinking about how he'd changed at the sight of Lucy, although he was already a grown man, in his early thirties, hard set in his ways. Since there wasn't anything else for Jack to do in the *kiva*, he took up the story for his audience of lizards: "She was purdy enough, but that wasn't the whole of it. When Lucy'd come laughing out of that movie house in downtown Winslow with her girlfriend in tow, she just tossed me a look as she passed—that was all she'd had to do—but it was like I'd been doused with kerosene and lit."

"She'd ducked her head down and said something to her friend, but I still heard her make that comment about my hat. Truth be told, it provoked me. I handed Fred the scrap of paper that listed the provisions we'd come into town for and rode her down. 'What's wrong with my hat?' I'd asked her—just like that, I come out with it. And Lucy had smiled in that sweet way she had and explained she was new in these parts and hadn't had the opportunity of meeting a real cowboy before, and well, was I one? 'Well, hell, yes, I'm real,' I'd told her, and I'd offered up my arm for her to pinch. She did it, too, and I howled and made her laugh. We went on and on after that, until the girlfriend, I think it her name was Margie, got tired of standing around with her hands on her hips and pulled Lucy away."

That was the only reason they'd had to stop talking, there on the sidewalk that day. And all those polite words had come out of a man with no real friends and a habit, when he did come to town, of crossing the street to avoid having to meet the eyes of the women walking toward him.

But Lucy was special. She was from back east, Ohio, Jack learned after bugging Margie at the bank the next day. She'd run away at twenty-four from an over-protective mother and come to live with her friend Margie in the wild west. Margie had told Jack where Lucy was working—as a secretary for one of the lawyers in town—and Jack had hurried right over there like he knew what he was doing, like he'd already figured out that this was the woman he was going to talk into marrying him. "And I done just that; it didn't even take me very long."

"Lucy couldn't cook worth a damn—she said her mother hadn't wanted her underfoot in the kitchen—and she was a city girl, through and through, scared of the cattle and horses and rough-looking men that make up a ranch." Later, after they'd stopped talking, Jack would sit across the table from her, silently wondering why the hell they had married each other, and it was her reasons that confused him the most. Why was she submitting to this daily torture? Katie had been a colicky baby, and she'd wake them both up several times every night until they were sleep-walking through their separate lives. Now the only time

Lucy smiled was when she was reading or working in her garden, and those were private pleasures that Jack wasn't even meant to see.

The patch of sunlight on the ground was starting to angle toward the eastern wall of the *kiva* when Jack carefully pulled his leg up onto the bench and lay on his back, one arm over his eyes. He was plumbing memories now that had been buried so long they were dustier than the photographs in Katie's bottom drawer. Because before the silence there had been the most pleasant banter Jack had ever engaged in—that's what had set Lucy apart from all the other women he'd ever met. Even that first day, they'd tossed lines back and forth like they'd known each other for years. And at the lawyer's office, Jack had had trouble keeping up with her—and he'd never been slow in the yack department.

It was the quick come-back Lucy was so good at. Jack would say something and she'd have some quirky response, ready to go, that made him pull up short and think again. Like the time he'd asked her out for a nice, juicy steak—he remembered his mouth had been watering in anticipation—and she'd rattled off twenty-four reasons for not eating meat. She said things—telling naughty jokes like they was nothing, or naming a women's private parts out loud, for instance—that shocked him. This dainty gal could make him gasp, and he'd hung around some of the crustiest, bad-mouthed old cowboys still working the range. He'd watched Fred back away from her, bright red with embarrassment, at the string of obscenities she'd leveled at the prickly pear that had dared to catch at her skirt. Then the next minute she was using book language that took him several heartbeats to translate, but when he did reply, she was already turning the words around on him again somehow. Once she'd said, "Jack Junior, you are as obdurate as any of your cattle," and after a gape-mouthed pause he'd stuttered what he hoped was a suitable response: "Hell, woman, I was just thinking . . . ." And she'd popped out, "Well those thoughts you are so busy chewing seem a lot more stubborn than most cud."

What the hell *had* she meant, anyway, Jack wondered. She made fun of him, all the time, poking him in the gut and laughing to make sure he caught the joke, and he loved it. ("Beans last night for dinner *and* beans for breakfast? You best ride your slowest steed or stay well down wind of your little cowboy buddies today, mister.") She seldom ventured further from the house than the porch—she'd sit out there for hours with her nose in a book or sewing on something—but she had an opinion about every decision Jack would make about running the ranch ("Yes, call the vet. Fifty bucks now means the damn cow lives to bring herself and a slew more calves to market. Get on the damn phone!") He'd usually gripe the whole time he did exactly as she'd said because she was right—what she said generally made sense, once he thought about it. The world was a different place through Lucy's eyes, through her darting mind; it excited him, and he wanted to live in that world with her forever.

That was the last reason Jack had moved by himself into the trailer. Growing up, Katie had never said much of anything to him; she had submitted to almost every discussion with her eyes averted, answering him sullenly, waiting for him to finish talking and turn his attention to something else. But once Richard was in the picture all that changed. During their courtship the two of them would sit together at the kitchen table, sparring amicably, long after Jack had taken his after-dinner whiskey into the living room with him, intending to read the newspaper. He'd lie on the couch, eavesdropping with his eyes closed, and drift off to sleep listening to Katie flatter and bully and tease Richard until the young man was just as besotted as Jack had been by her mother.

It made him proud of her but kind of sad, too. After their marriage, Jack had had to get out of there. Not because he was jealous—that wasn't it. It was because he was afraid it would stop, and he was starting to realize, lying there on that rocky slab, that there were some losses he wouldn't be able to survive twice.

Jack jolted awake, his heart hammering. *No sense in panicking*, he told himself. *That won't help none.* He folded his hands on his chest to help himself stop breathing so hard. *Think about Katie.* Now that she was pregnant she reminded Jack of how his wife Lucy had looked with her thin frame ballooned out in the front, her small breasts turning into the generous bust of some other woman. Lucy's face had filled out some, too, and her cheeks had taken on that same healthy glow.

Jack groaned, licked at his cracked lips. *Go on with the story.* Little Kate was born in the winter, and Jack and Lucy spent the best part of her nine-month gestation digging up the backyard and making one hell of a garden together, bigger than their little family and a few ranch hands would ever need. "But Lucy was hot on learning how to can, and she'd mastered the art of boiling water by then, so we had all kinds of steamed vegetables every night, slathered with butter, plus a thick slab of beef for me, of course." He laughed. "I gained pret' near every pound she did." It made his stomach growl, just thinking about it.

He didn't remember the second pregnancy nearly as well. Lucy'd started ordering magazines after Katie was born. At first they were all about parenting and home-making, but then she added all kinds of glossy fashion mags and travel digests, and he was getting the message that she wanted, more than anything, to be someone else, somewhere else. When Jack came in from a dawn to dust workday he'd be lucky if she'd point, without raising her eyes, to where his dinner waited, burned and dry, on the stove. Otherwise she'd be bouncing a howling baby on her hip, which was only worse—Jack couldn't take all that caterwauling; he just wasn't used to it. Sometimes he'd turn around right in the doorway and head back out to ride through the silence under the stars.

He had plenty of silence now—a couple of flies buzzing around the dead snake, his own breathing, the gasps that escaped him when he tried to move. It was too quiet; he dozed and woke again, pushed himself to think, to focus on something besides his thirst, his hunger, welcoming even the jolts of pain as a distraction. God, was he thirsty.

Lucy's lying in for their second child had started off wrong and gone bad from there. The labor began early, for one thing, nearly a month ahead of schedule. And her water broke right away; Jack remembered waking up wet in the bed beside her, and he'd stomped off, mad about it, to get the midwife.

Then things slowed down after that; the contractions went on and on but hours later there was still no baby. The midwife hadn't insisted that they take Lucy in to the hospital until almost an hour after Jack had stopped pacing in the hallway and left to drive a buyer—who'd come all the way from Topeka, Kansas—through the herd. By the time his foreman had tracked them down and Jack had rushed back to the house, Lucy was giving dry birth to a worn out little boy with unformed lungs who breathed one raspy, old-man breath in Jack's arms and then died.

Lucy hadn't wanted to look at the boy—or maybe it was Jack she grimaced at and turned her face away from. He couldn't even try to comfort her, with this dead baby in his arms, and with the midwife and neighbor women forming a moving wall around the bed.

What did Katie remember of all that, Jack wondered suddenly. *She'd been real little, but . . . . And now with her being pregnant herself?*

Lucy hadn't been well enough to attend the funeral, so Jack had stood alone at the baby's graveside in the family plot with his good black felt hat in his hands, listening to the comments the little group of people muttered as they disbanded, about what a shame it was, in this day and age, to let a baby die that way. He might have lived, had they been in the hospital, had they not been living so far from town and if all of them weren't so fearful of doctors and outsiders in general. Or maybe nobody said those things but only thought them so loudly that Jack had to squeeze his eyes shut and shake his head to clear the words out of his ears.

Jack did remember yelling at Katie for getting her new dress dirty; the whole time the preacher had been talking she'd been digging a burrow under the oak tree that stood in a corner of the family graveyard. He'd yanked her by the hand and half-dragged her the two hundred yards back to the house, thinking black and bitter thoughts. He knew, already, that Lucy had quit on him, that this little girl was the only child—the only future—he'd ever have.

Jack heard the dog come back. When Hud whined down into the *kiva* it dawned on Jack that the mutt had not eaten all day, either. Then the Lab raised his head and howled out a long, musical note. Jack knew exactly what that frosted black muzzle looked like, pointed at the sky, narrow lips pursed; one of their hands, Tom, liked to carry around a harmonica in his back pocket, and from time to time he'd pull it out and blow a tune. If Hud was anywhere within ear-shot, he'd hurry over, plant himself at the wrangler's feet, and howl out notes of varying pitch in accompaniment. Only this time the dog kept hitting one long, mournful note, again and again, proceeded by a series of sharp yips, until Jack could no longer resist the urge to join him.

"Please, please, please," Jack yelped as loudly as he could, then "help me-e-e-e-e, help me-e-e-e-e," he wailed. After a moment spent thinking about his daughter, about how much like her mother she'd turned out, and about how bad things did happen, even in hospitals, even now-a-days, he sang out, "Help us. Help us all-l-l-l-l-o-o-o-o."

THIRTY

I cleaned myself up the best I could in the downstairs bathroom, leaving streaks of soot on the hand towel—I just couldn't drag myself up those stairs to do a proper job—and decided I'd sneak some of the coffee Richard had made while he was outside showing the girl around the stable yard. I waddled into the kitchen and was startled again—I'd forgotten Paula was still in there. She was shuffling a pile of papers back into her battered leather briefcase. Then she had to jump up and help me to a seat at the table as another contraction hit.

"Goodness," she gasped, "shouldn't you be getting to the hospital?"

"It's early," I told her as soon as I could talk again. "A good three weeks. Maybe they'll go away."

She tilted her head at me, looking doubtful, then watched me hoist myself up and cross the kitchen to the cupboard. I pulled down a bowl and a box of cereal, then I remembered my manners—we didn't do much entertaining in this house. "Can I get you anything?" She was shaking her head. "Coffee, at least?" But then I saw Richard had already poured her a cup. I found a spoon in the drainer in the sink, got the milk out of the refrigerator.

"You're good people to give Jane a chance here," Paula said as I sat back down to eat. "She's a really clever kid, but she's had a rough start."

"Uh-huh," I said with my mouth full. For some reason I kept the girl's confidence—her name—to myself.

"She's got family, if you want to call it that, down in Cave Creek. But it was a bad enough environment that she ran away, and then they—well, let's just say it was decided Jane was better off here. So as a ward of the state, she needs to hold down some kind of job—and stay in school, of course." Paula said all this brightly, like it was a normal rite of passage for a child—this young—to be so at odds with the world. "She adores your husband. I'm sure she's going to be on her best behavior."

That wasn't helping me place much trust in the kid, either. What was her less-than-best behavior, I wondered. Maybe Dad had been right—maybe this was a bad idea. Then I noticed Richard through the kitchen window. He was talking to Fred with his hands moving emphatically, already turning toward the house. The phone rang just as he bounded up the steps and through the door.

"Yes?" he demanded of the receiver, still in motion, pacing the hallway to the end of the phone cord. "Yes, he's my father-in-law. . . . Richard Crawford. It's the Navajo Tribal police," he told me in a stage whisper, a hand over the receiver.

I lumbered up, my heart in my throat, but he was listening and wouldn't look at me, although I took his shirt in both of my hands and kept saying, "What? What?"

"How bad?" he asked, and then I really went crazy, pulling on the receiver. "Oh, Jeez. Yeah. Well, can we put out a missing-persons? Just a minute, Kate. You're kidding. . . . Yeah. I see. Well, look for a dog, too—a black Lab. We think he took him with him. Okay, let me write this down." He scribbled "Ganado" and a phone number on the pad by the phone, but I had to go sit down at the table. It wasn't another contraction—I was just too dizzy to stand. Then I couldn't help it—I started crying again.

Richard hung up, then he brought the pad into the kitchen with him. "Kate, honey, you need to calm down. They found the truck," he told me. He drew a breath like he had to steal himself to go on: "on its side in a ditch near Ganado."

"Oh, Jesus," I wailed, but Richard shook his head.

"Kate, just relax. He said it didn't look too bad. The windshield's intact, no blood or anything—just a bunch of beer cans and Jack's hat. They think he must have caught a ride somewhere."

"What would Dad be doing on the Reservation?" I asked myself out loud, wiping at my face. Paula was watching all this drama with her mouth open.

"Well, right, that's a good question." Richard turned to Paula, explaining, "Kate's father's missing, since last night." He was using his "teacher voice," all calm and collected, and I couldn't tell if it was for my benefit or hers. "Anyway, the truck's been towed to the impound yard. They've notified the Sherriff here, and once we file some kind of missing adult waiver form—I thought we did that last night, but they don't have it yet—they'll organize a search for him."

"No, I'm not waiting, Richard," I insisted, pulling him by the shirt front down to my eye level. "*You* have to go find him. Now."

"How?" he asked, cutting short a nervous laugh. "Katie, sweetheart, you must be aware of the fact that we're having a baby right now."

"I could be in labor for days, Richard. There's plenty of time. You have to go."

"Go where? No. Kate, all they've got is an empty truck."

I let him go and wept into my hands, thinking about how exhausted I must be to be crying like this in front of a stranger. Richard tried to hug me, tried to get me to stop. "I'm not leaving you, Kate," he said into my hair. "I'm sure he's on his way home right now. And if he's not back, after we're through this, after the baby's here . . . ."

"But that could be too late!"

"I might know someone who can help," Paula said, making us both look up. She moved around in her chair, obviously uncomfortable, but went on. "Normally I wouldn't suggest such a thing—and please don't say anything at the school, Richard. Okay? But I have an uncle, a . . . wise man. A 'hand trembler.' He's been at my aunt's this past week. He's . . . he has a gift."

* * * * *

Richard considered himself a scientist—at least, a social scientist—and any kind of hocus-pocus made him squirm, so I know he agreed to follow Paula to her aunt's house mostly because Paula's aunt lived in Winslow. He made me promise I would make our visit short and then we'd go straight on to the hospital. We called a good-bye to *Tio* Fred from the driveway—he looked kind of like a robot with that bulky, white cast cradled against his chest—and Richard shouted, "We'll call you, soon as we know anything," across the yard. The girl looked up but kept on messing with Summer over the corral fence as we drove off; she had a hose sunk in the water trough. Richard saw me ducking to watch her in the side view mirror and said, "They'll be fine. Jane really has a thing for horses. You should have seen her when we walked into the barn. One look at Ol' Midnight and, I don't know, she kinda lost it. But in a good way," he assured me hurriedly when I turned to him, frowning. I didn't mention the girl's real name to him, either. I suppose I should have. She was his student, after all.

But I had other, more important things on my mind. Most of my life I've lived in a kind of haze, I was starting to realize, mooning over characters in books or memories or daydreams, but since the sky had turned orange, since Dad had disappeared, I was in major here-and-now mode. What I wanted most was to know what that crazy father of mine was up to. Even impending labor couldn't top that, though Richard obviously was prioritizing differently; every time I shifted in the car seat he'd turn to me with alarm. He'd put a plastic garbage bag over the seat and a bath towel over that; I think he was a little afraid that the baby was going to pop out while we were driving. But the contractions were still spaced well apart, and I would focus on that later. Right now I knew that what Paula had offered up at our kitchen table was a chance—a long shot, granted—to see through the confusion of what we think we know or don't know or should or shouldn't know and glimpse what was. I wasn't any sort of scientist, and I was desperate. Dad had never done anything this stupid before. And June on the rez meant hot and dry days, cool nights. If he was out there somewhere I had to find him—soon.

Paula had said her uncle was not a witch or even a medicine man but what they call a "hand trembler." His gift for seeing the causes of diseases and disharmony came from the spirit of the Gila Monster, she'd explained, tapping her chest. She was clearly embarrassed to talk about it, but the Navajo are like that; they're protective of their cultural traditions and wary of outsiders, but if you do well by them—and apparently offering Rose a job had been a benefit to Paula somehow—then they'll go all out to repay you. Her only concern was that this uncle had come off the rez to diagnose the illness of a family member, and she knew he was going back today. When she'd said that I'd told Richard to splash some water on his face, grab a muffin out of the pantry, and get the keys. After all that stalling I was raring to go.

Paula finally pulled into the driveway of a small, cement block house in an older Winslow neighborhood just down from the grade school, and we parked at the curb. As we walked up the drive—Richard had me by the arm like I was some kind of invalid—Paula gestured at the truck beside her car. "That's a good sign," she said. "He should still be here."

It had been a while since the last contraction, but then a pretty big one hit, and I had to stop there between the vehicles for a minute while Paula went in to arrange for our visit. "Don't get your hopes up, honey," Richard told me, his hand on my shoulder. "It's going to be pretty hard for anyone—including Paula's uncle—to tell us where Jack's sleeping it off this time. Your dad just might have to find his own way home."

"He's too old," I countered, shrugging his hand away, "and too sick." I was mad because Richard can be just as bad as my father; he was so stubborn sometimes. Other people have told me they admire Richard's integrity, but they don't have to live with the down side of his determination to do what's "logical." I knew there was no way to change his mind when he got like this, but if he had wanted to make me happy he'd already be out searching for my father.

Richard looked over his shoulder at the house, sighing. "Well, it seems he's still well enough to go out on a hell of a binge. Your dad's got a lot of ornery left in him yet, Kate—years of it, I'd say."

Paula came to the door and motioned us in. I pushed myself forward, and I wouldn't let Richard take my arm to help me into the house. Paula introduced us to her aunt—a woman who was probably in her sixties, with striking white lines through her black hair—and gestured at the couch. But after I watched Richard sink into its cushions I chose one of the hard-backed chairs, instead. Then Paula's uncle came down the hallway to greet us.

Richard rose to shake hands but the older man just smiled and gestured for him to sit back down. "Thank you, *Hosteen*, for seeing us," Richard said. I understood why Richard used the title of respect, but at the same time I wasn't sure this was an old man. He was tiny—shorter than me—and moved purposefully but without any sign of infirmity, and his eyes, although nearly swallowed by the wrinkles on his face, were a youngster's eyes. Paula moved one of the chairs closer and her uncle sat beside me. I smiled at him nervously, completely at a loss.

"You're looking for someone," he told me. I was barely aware of Paula's aunt asking Richard if he'd like some ice tea and then turning to me, the same question in her eyes, but I only glanced at her. I was captivated by the old Navajo beside me—his hair was cropped so short you could see the shape of his skull, like a boy's or even a baby's small, round, nearly hairless globe. I heard Richard responding, "Thanks anyway. We've actually got only a little time. We're having a baby."

"My father. He didn't come home last night, but they found his truck near Ganado, and he set the trailer. . . ."

Paula's uncle held up a weathered hand, and I looked at his fingers to see if they were going to tremble. Instead, his eyes rolled back in his head, and I decided he *was* old, ancient, in fact, maybe eighty or ninety. He sniffed, then wrinkled his nose. In a kind voice he said: "This *Bilagáana* is not well. He smells bad."

"Oh, my God," I whimpered, looking at Richard. But he was distracted; he was watching Paula speaking in Navajo to her aunt, gesturing toward me.

"Don't be too worried," the old man reassured me. "I've smelled a lot worse." He still had his head tilted back, his eyes open and sightless. "Here," he said, placing a hand on his belly. "Here, too." He patted his left thigh. Then he nodded his head, smiling: "Look in the mesas, but down, below the ground."

"Is he dead?" I gasped, but the old man closed his eyes and his gap-toothed smile widened.

"Oh, no. I can hear him talking."

I heard Richard chuckle softly on the couch.

"Is he alone?" I asked.

The old man shook his head, no. "He has his best friend with him," he assured me. He opened his eyes and stood up, and I realized the interview was over.

"Thank you," I told him, although I still had no idea what anything he had just said meant.

"There's no need to thank me," he said, "but you can give my sister something, if you wish, for gasoline. The poor girl has been taking me everywhere lately, haven't you?" Richard rose from the couch and pulled his wallet out of his pocket, but the old man was still focused on me. "Here—let me give you something, too," he said.

Most of the old man's teeth were missing but his smile was delightfully mischievous. He spoke to Paula in Navajo and she left the room briefly, then returned with a beaded cedar nut necklace dangling from her fingers. "For your daughter," the old man told me with a wink, and he closed it in my palm.

THIRTY-ONE

The night I killed Tristan was this day's opposite: even though it had been only early evening when I barreled him out of the stable yard, the sky had been black with a nightmare of a rain storm, the worst monsoon ever, crazy loud with wind and thunder and pounding rain, drenching the desert that had been baking dry for months and flipping us all from drought to flood in the flash of a lightning strike.

It's hard to believe that was only about a year ago. I had been miserable, practically catatonic because Guy was gone, first after they'd locked him up for assaulting Frank, even though the fat asshole had totally deserved the beating for selling our Arabians right out from under us. I honestly don't think Guy meant to kill him, but I wouldn't have blamed him even if he had. Fat assholes with bad hearts shouldn't get in brawls with younger men; you'd think even a jerk like Frank would have been smart enough to know that. Still Guy must have felt really bad about it because after four months in jail he just disappeared; all last summer he was just missing, evaporated into the desert somehow. Nobody even talked about him, not even his friend, Manny, who kept things going around the stable. Certainly not Lily. She seemed relieved, even, and way too busy bossing Manny and Luis around, now that she was in charge of the whole damn show, and landing herself a new boyfriend.

She tried to boss me, but I wasn't having it. Besides the new boyfriend there were lawyers coming around the place, Frank's sister was all pissed off and calling the house every other day, and I told the bitch if she hired another trainer or messed with any of Guy's stuff in the trainer's house I was gonna give them all an earful about her sleeping around and stuff. So Lily backed off and I kept going—I kept following what Guy had said the plan was, and I got Tristan saddle-trained as best I could. And I kept myself alive by telling myself that Tristan needed me and by holding onto the hope that Guy would come back.

And then he did, as suddenly as if the wind that was driving that storm down on us had blown him back. But he was different, somehow, I don't know, just *calm* in this weird way. And he kept his cool despite the way I threw myself on him when I found him packing his stuff in the trainer's house, even with the hurry-the-fuck-up urgency of that wind screaming through the curtains, the crazy-odd smell of rain in the air. We could have done it, in that storm we *could* have taken that horse—*his* horse, I'd heard Lily say Tristan was rightfully his—and gotten away. He could have saved us.

Instead he turned on me; he lied right to my face, trying to trick me. He said to get my stuff together like he really was going to take me and Tristan with him. I had wanted that so f-ing much for so f-ing long that I actually fell for it until I was outside and saw Manny leading Lily over and thought about the suitcase Guy had been trying to hide from me. There was a rolled up blanket in Manny's truck bed, and I just *knew* what it was for—and that it meant Guy was punking out on his plan to claim his horse, after all.

So *I* took him, instead. I grabbed the bedroll, and I screamed at Guy when he followed me out to the porch. I shouted: "You f-ing don't deserve him, anyway," and I ran for the show barn, for Tristan's stall, not bothering with a saddle just yanking at the latch, scaring the horse against the back wall. I saw the hand-made bridle spill out of the blanket when I tossed it down and took the chance that the ten seconds spent wrestling that over Tristan's poll would still give me time enough to get away. When Guy came in I was up on that horse in a flash and running over him, then hanging on—I thought for sure Tristan was going to dump me when he reared—but I hung on, and then we were tearing down the lane into that freakin' storm. The rain was pounding us so hard it hurt to raise my head so I just shut my eyes and let the horse go until I heard the car brakes squeal, the horn blare, then I reined him toward the mountains.

We were flying past fences, dogs racing against us on the other side, barking, then we started weaving through bushes and cacti, and I just gripped the halter and a handful of mane and hunched against the constant pelting, the cracks of lightning right overheard, the deafening booms. When we made the golf course Tristan launched into a full-out gallop, spraying clods of dirt, then suddenly he snorted and dug in, reared. I was on my but in the mud before I'd even thought about falling, and I looked up just as he skidded into the flooded wash, and I watched as the waves and branches and swirling chunks of bushes roared right over him. He screamed—I'm haunted by that last, terrified, oh, God—I still can't . . . . I hate thinking about it. Then he was gone, pulled under, swept away.

I scrambled up and took off without even stopping to think about where I was going. Eventually I stumbled onto some blacktop and stuck my thumb out. And here I am.

THIRTY-TWO

As He Who Cuts the Life Out of the Enemy and Monster Slayer followed the long trail home, the children of every village they passed through would see them coming from a long way off. The sun was throwing splinters of light from their helmets in rays around their heads; their bright armor and sharp knives added to the glow. The children would call out to their elders to come see this amazing sight, and in each place the young men would tell the story of the Big Giant's demise at their hands as they showed off his shaggy scalp. Then they would eat and drink whatever the women of that village placed at their feet. "Well done!" the people would remark at the end of their tale. "You are both brave and strong and worthy of many victory songs!"

But as the men approached their own home Monster Slayer stopped. He took off his helmet and hid it under a bush. Beside it he placed his battle armor and his weapons. He Who Cuts the Life Out of the Enemy saw him doing this and hid his own arms in the same place. Over it all he laid their prize; the monster's hair made the pile look like a messy, overgrown shrub.

They both looked up at the sound of their mothers' excited voices. "My son! My son!" Changing Woman was calling as she ran to meet them. "Where have you been? We were very afraid for both of you!"

"We were sure the alien monsters had eaten you!" White Shell Woman added breathlessly as she joined them. But she did not pull her son into her arms as she would have only days before. Something made her keep her hands at her side.

Monster Slayer stood up tall and answered them in a strong voice: "We have followed the path that Spider Woman said would lead us to our father, the Sun, to ask for his help. Then we traveled to the Blue Bead Mountain. There we destroyed *Yé'iitsoh*, the Big Giant."

Changing Woman gasped and placed her hand over her mouth. White Shell Woman looked over her shoulder nervously, saying,

"Children, do not joke like this. If he hears you, we will *all* be devoured!"

Monster Slayer smiled at their fear. "Come," he said gently. "See." And he led them to their hidden trophies. He Who Cuts the Life Out of the Enemy removed the giant's scalp with a flourish, exposing the glittering pile of their helmets and weapons.

The women stepped back in wonder. They glanced at one another, then they turned with new respect to the boys who had returned to them as men. A victory song came soaring out of White Shell Woman's throat, and the four of them, arm in arm, danced.

THIRTY-THREE

Dozing, Jack worked Maggie through the crush of cattle in the portable corral, tossing a flat-handed loop at the feet of the steer he wanted and catching its heels. Maggie knew to set back as Jack took a few dallies around his pommel and the steer hopped a step, then stretched its boney back to its limit. Chuck was at the steer's side in an instant, jabbing an injection under the bawling bovine's skin just as Jack urged Maggie forward to put the slack back in the lariat. The steer was free several seconds before he moved, turning his ears this way and that, looking for Chuck, who was already back at the fence line, reaching into the cooler for another loaded syringe.

Jack and Maggie hazed the vaccinated steer toward the shoot Fred had just stepped away from, and it clambered up into the stock truck with its brethren. Fred gave it a nice pat on its flank with his coiled *reata* and returned to his position at the gate while Jack and Maggie picked another steer to trip up. That little spotted one with the patch of hair sticking straight up between its ears made a fine target. It went on like this all day, a dance of horse and beef and beef-eaters, a rhythmic repetition of moves and evasions, capture and release, repeated dozens of times until all the cattle they'd gathered that day were loaded for their ride north to summer pasture.

But in his dreaming the work never ended. The flies that were tickling Jack's nose, the dust nearly closing his throat, the dull throbbing of his leg were incorporated into an unceasing sorting—mama cows and the calves too young to wean had to go in one corral, the yearling calves needing ear marks, vaccinations, and castration in this other one. Steers had to be pushed and hollered into the alley between the two and tallied as they charged down the chute. Eight head, fifteen head, twenty-nine head, thirty-six head, but then he lost track and started the count over again, but the steers were milling around in the corral, now, tossing their heads, raising a cloud of confusion over their swaying rumps, until one turned, eyeing Jack, on the fight, tail whipping, pawing earth, hooking its head like it still owned the horns that would gut Maggie, dethrone Jack, and set the man up for the raging steer's final satisfaction.

Jack woke himself, moaning, and struggled to sit up, glad to be freed from the nightmare. The beasts he'd husbanded had not loved him, and rightly so. None of their interactions with man had been pleasant. In the delirium of pain and pain-killers Jack made another vow: he'd set the critters free. He'd hang up his spurs, a cattleman no more. If he lived, he was finished. He was through.

THIRTY-FOUR

I gave my full legal name—Kathleen Ann Rawlings—on the hospital admittance form, thinking that, if something should happen—God forbid—the document would need to be correct, even though it meant Richard's last name wasn't included. I didn't ask him what he thought—he was pacing the corridor behind me and being of absolutely no help, and I'd already called him over twice to help me answer a question on the form. But he had this dazed look on his face, and he couldn't remember the name of the birthing class we'd gone to or even how to spell the weird name of the doctor we'd selected as the baby's pediatrician. Now he whirled around just as a nurse was rolling a patient past him in a wheel chair and he nearly ended up on the old guy's lap. "Rich," I said, and he stopped apologizing and hurried over to take my arm.

"Are you all right? Are you having another contraction?" His face was almost comical, his eyebrows drawn down with concern, and I wondered how in the hell he was going to get through this.

"You've got to sign here," I told him, handing him the pen, "if you're going to own this child." Then I watched him push the hank of hair out of his eyes and adjust his glasses, scanning the form before he wrote his name. I was hoping the baby would get his looks—my brains, though, not that Richard wasn't a smart man. He married me, didn't he?

Then I really was having another contraction and Richard started bossing people around. He snapped his fingers at the admitting nurse until she came back to the counter and took the form away, and he held onto me with one arm and waved the other one around while he complained loudly about having to wait before they'd admit me to triage. I was counting, trying not to tense up, but Richard's bicep against my ribs was hard as a rock. The nurse said we could have picked up the form early and completed it at home, so Richard said, "Well, we're early, all right? We didn't know it was going to be this early."

An orderly showed up then and took us a little ways down the hall, opening a door to the triage area. I looked over my shoulder, thinking about apologizing to the admitting nurse but she was too busy rolling her eyes and shaking her head at my husband's back.

In the triage area another nurse was sitting at a little desk, filling out a different form. The orderly pulled a curtain aside, led me into a little cubicle, and helped me onto the bed, and I realized I was excited, really happy to be there. But the nurse acted like I'd interrupted her coffee break or something. "Your contractions are how far apart?" she asked. I had lost track during the drive to town and our visit with Paula's uncle, so I kind of shrugged, and Richard had his head down in his hands like he hadn't even heard the question.

"Has your water broken?" she asked. "Have you seen the mucus plug? Any bleeding or vaginal discharge?" I shook my head, no, no, no. She took my blood pressure and temperature, then drew the curtain shut and did a visual exam. "The cervix is partially effaced, and you're two centimeters dilated. Are your contractions getting stronger?" She kind of tsked at me when I said I'd been a little distracted and I wasn't really sure. "Call me when the next contraction starts," she drawled on her way out.

Richard finally pulled his head up when she left. "What's that supposed to mean?" he asked. Then he turned to me. "What are we waiting for now?"

I just shrugged again and then lay back, my hands on the sides of the mountain rising out of my middle. "I've figured out the best friend part—that's got to be Hud, right? But what did he mean, 'look under the ground'? You think there's—what?—sinkholes or open graves out there, maybe?"

"Well, I guess the mesas could be made of limestone," Richard said, standing up and trying to find room to pace in the tiny cubicle. "But there's not enough water to make a sinkhole. And it's not a grave—the *Diné* have all kinds of prohibitions about dealing with the dead, and there's no way your dad would be allowed anywhere near their cemeteries." He stopped to move a chair out of his way. "It would really help if we had even a glimmer of an idea about why he was there in the first place."

"How are we doing?" the nurse asked.

I sighted her over the mound of my belly and said, "Fine," in a small voice. Great, now that people were waiting on me I'd probably get stage fright and the labor would just stop.

"Let me know as soon as the next contraction starts," she said again and her head disappeared.

"I was wondering if there might be caves up there in the mesas," Richard said, taking three steps and turning. "I could see your dad holin' up somewhere for a last big fight, couldn't you? And Paula's uncle said, 'look in the mesas,' right?"

"I don't know, Rich. Even Dad's not that much of a romantic. I mean, he blusters, but—naw. It's gotta be some kind of accident—maybe an open mine?"

Richard stopped and pointed at me. "Maybe," he said, then he yelled, "Hey, Nurse!" because he could see by my face that the next contraction had finally hit.

But my measly contractions of a half minute's duration at ten minute intervals just weren't good enough for her. "We usually don't admit patients until the contractions are closer to five minutes apart. Or until their water breaks," she said. "You're not quite through the thirty-seventh week, so the baby's just short of full term. It could be false labor."

"There's nothing false about those contractions," Richard interjected, but the nurse just smiled at him.

"I called your doctor. He's in another delivery right now, but he'll probably want to examine you. Why don't you wait in the lobby for a while and we'll see how things develop." She was really friendly now that she was helping me up off the bed and leading me to the hallway. Richard was hanging back like he didn't want to go.

I took it as a sign. "Give me some quarters," I insisted, and I waited impatiently for Richard to dig the coins out of his pocket, then I waddled across the hospital lobby to the pay phone.

I called our own number first and got no one. Of course Fred and the kid were probably nowhere near the house phone, but I let it ring on and on, hoping one of them would hear it. I was glad Paula had said she'd run out to the ranch first thing tomorrow to check on how they were doing. A runaway using an alias who freaks out when she sees a black stallion—what had I gotten us into? So I got my quarters back and was able to reach the sheriff and, yes, he'd heard about the truck from the Navajo Tribal Police. In fact, he'd sent a deputy up to Ganado, and they were kind of surprised he hadn't come across Dad trying to hitch-hike home.

Then I started to call the Winslow city police but I hung up when another contraction started. I looked around for Richard and spotted him on the other side of the lobby, looking longingly at something through the gift shop window. When I got my breath back I dialed the Winslow police department, but the officer made it sound like it was a big deal to have to recheck his drunk tank, and when he finally came back to the phone he said nobody by Dad's name or description had been incarcerated. He was the one who told me to check the hospital, so I hung up and tried to get that nurse at the counter to talk to me again.

"He's disappeared," I sighed as I sank onto the plastic cushion next to Richard.

"You called the sheriff?" he asked me. His eyes were at half-mast, and I remembered neither of us had gotten much sleep last night. "Did you tell him what Paula's uncle said?"

"No," I said, smiling. "You think I should have?"

He shrugged. "It's not much to go on, anyway." He watched me wince and change my position on the couch. "I guess we should be keeping a better record of these," he said over the noise of my breathing, but he barely glanced at his watch. "When's Chuck supposed to be back?"

"Tomorrow or the next day," I told him. It was unusual for Richard to worry about the ranch and things like when our foreman was due back—that was Dad's job, and it gave me a jolt, I don't know, like a longing. But all I said was: "If this is Wednesday. Is this Wednesday? I've kind of lost track."

"Yeah," Richard said. He was looking off toward that gift shop again, and finally he came out with it. "They've got one of our pregnancy books in there—you know, the one with the pink cover. I think I might buy it."

"Richard, why would you want to buy a book we already own?" But when he looked at me kind of sheepishly I knew why.

"I never read the last chapters," he said anyway. "I was kind of saving them. I thought I had time," he added, because I was shaking my head. Then he said: "I'm not ready for this."

"Well, too bad," I told him. I rocked forward on the couch and lumbered to my feet. I was mad because I felt stuck on the edge of everything: I knew my dad was out there somewhere, but I couldn't for the life of me seem to find him; on the other hand, I knew exactly where this baby was, but I didn't seem to be doing a very good job of getting him out.

Then my thighs were wet and the inside of my legs tickled as the drops worked their way down. It wasn't exactly Niagara Falls, but I knew with a certainty that doesn't come from books that it was amniotic fluid starting a puddle in my shoe. "It's show time," I told Richard, holding out my hand. I was surprised at how bright his eyes were. He really was scared, I realized, and, for a change, I wasn't afraid at all.

THIRTY-FIVE

Okay, I'm f-ing freaking out. It's just past dark, and there's all these creepy f-ing noises coming from different rooms in this big, old house like there's ghosts dancing around upstairs or something, and that old Mexican guy already came up here once and poked his head in all the rooms and told me it was nothing—or rather, he said: *No es nada*, which I'm pretty sure means "it's nothing"—and now I'm thinking he's already gone to bed—the light down there in the bunkhouse just went out—and I'm all f-ing alone out here with a whole bunch of ghosts in the middle of bum-fuck Egypt. I don't even know the phone number of the group home, or Paula, or I would have called them like an hour ago because I wish to hell they'd come get me.

I don't know what I was thinking, coming out here. It wasn't bad earlier when Mr. C. called from the hospital and had me run over and get Fred. After they'd talked Fred brought me back to the bunk house with him for the supper he'd cooked us on his old wood stove. The cheese and beans he'd wrapped up in a tortilla tasted good, and he wasn't chatty, just let me poke around in the box of bridle pieces and worn lariats and broken spurs and scraps of leather he has on the table beside his bed, a regular cowboy jigsaw puzzle.

But then it started: bam, bam, bam—there was a long pause, then bam, bam, bam. It stopped for a while again and then after it got quiet enough to hear the birds arguing in the big tree by the house, there it was again: bam, bam, BAM. I started hunching, rocking, in that chair by Fred's table and he must have noticed. He said, "Don't let Ol' Midnight bother you, *chica*. He gets *nervioso*—jumpy, no? He's okay." He even came over and put his good hand on my shoulder, but I had to get out of there then.

Old Fred followed me up to the house and showed me my room, patted my towels stacked by the bathroom sink, just repeating stuff Mr. C. had already told me about, and for a while I was okay, snooping around—Mrs. C has got like a gazillion books—and if I'd just stayed downstairs I might still be okay but I went up there when I thought I heard a door close and the window in one of the rooms was open and I could hear the stallion pounding the hell out of his stall again—bam, bam, bam, bam, bam—so I put my hands over my ears and came downstairs but that's when I heard the baby cry and women's voices so I went and got Fred and made *him* go up there and he came back downstairs looking kind of sad but saying there was nothing, *nada*, so he said to lock the door behind him and I'd be safe.

But I'm not safe. I hear that horse, I feel him like he's the blood pounding in my ears, and the floor boards keep creaking over my head, and I'm so f-ing alone that I miss even my stupid, f-ing sister-mom, and now the writing isn't even helping anymore. I'm giving up—I'm going. I'm getting the hell out of here.

THIRTY-SIX

Monster Slayer could not sleep. He got up and went to look at the stars. Who Cuts the Life Out of His Enemy had seemed happy to follow his mother back to their lodge and sit by their fire but Monster Slayer had felt sad as he watched them go. Now he was restless, pacing the patch of ground outside his mother's lodge, wishing he was back on the Big Giant's trail.

Finally he poked his head inside his mother's still-dark home and shouted, "Do you know where *Déélgééd* the Horned Monster lives?" Because he had decided that there were still plenty of monsters left for him to kill. In fact, he had come to believe that wiping out the monsters was the one thing that would make the jittery feelings that were bothering him go away.

Changing Woman raised her head to look at him. "Oh, son," she sighed. She sat up, rubbing her eyes. "Please do not go looking for the Horned Monster," she said wearily. "Can't you just be satisfied with what you've accomplished?"

"Tell me," Monster Slayer insisted. "Let Who Cuts the Life Out of His Enemy stay here and guard you women. I am named for a purpose." And then he would not let her sleep until Changing Woman told him the whereabouts of his next victim.

The Horned Monster was a great four-legged animal with a huge, razor-sharp rack of antlers like a deer's, but he was no match for Monster Slayer's lightning arrows. Monster Slayer brought a chunk of the creature's flesh back to his mother and immediately began pestering her again: "Now tell me where *Tsé nináhálééhké*, the Bird Monster, and all his chicks are hiding!" Because the Horned Monster's blood still on his hands was not enough for him.

Changing Woman felt great fear for her son, and not just because of the terrible danger going after the Rock Bird Monsters would put him in. But Monster Slayer would not be satisfied until she told him how to find them, and when he strutted back into her lodge at the end of the next day and presented her with two gigantic feathers the first words out of his mouth were: "Where is *Tsé dah hódzíiltálii*, Who Kicks People Off of Cliffs?"

And so it continued. Monster Slayer would pause in the slaughter only long enough to eat a meal and sleep for several hours, then Changing Woman would beg him, each time, not to go. But Monster Slayer had tasted blood. He wanted more.

THIRTY-SEVEN

A kind of slow panic had gripped Jack when the light coming in through the entrance hole started fading again. He'd howled and yelled for help as long and as loudly as he could, and Hud had joined him, barking down into the pit at Jack until the walls echoed. But it was no use; Jack's throat was worn out and before very long his shouts were coming out as whispers.

A chill descended with the dark and Jack started shaking. Even though he hugged himself hard and gritted his teeth he couldn't stop trembling. He had a hard time getting the container open, but he finally managed it and gagged down the last of the pain pills, then Jack swept the other medicines off the bench with the back of his hand and stretched out carefully on the stones. It came to him suddenly, when he saw his hands clasped on his vibrating chest: he could pray.

"God," he croaked, "I need you. The damn—I mean, the darn dog can't help me. Nobody's coming. I can't help myself, so it's just gotta be you. I'm sorry about all the crap I've done through the years. I know I've been mean to the girl, at times. But I've never hurt her, not on purpose, anyways. Maybe she thinks I loved them damn cows more'n her, but that ain't so. I had to work; a man's got to support his family, and that's the only way I knew how. Anyhow, I've officially retired, Lord—she'll be happy to hear that.

"But I am sorry for the meanness. I'm sorry I weren't a better father to her. My heart kinda froze up on me; I couldn't help that. I'd lost everything, 'ceptin' the ranch—and my little girl, of course.

"And if my boy dyin' was my fault, I'm sorry for that, too. Ah, Lucy, you're the one I should've asked to forgive me, I guess." Jack swallowed back the acids burning their way up his throat. "Well, it's a damn sight too late for that. And if you're trying to put me in hell for it, Lord—well, you missed."

He stopped when he realized that, not only was God probably not listening, something else was missing, too. It had been quiet, too quiet, overhead for some time. Jack lay there shaking and listening for the dog; he was afraid if he called him, Hud wouldn't come and then he would know he was gone. But after another long wait, he knew it anyway. So Jack rose, groaning, onto his elbows, and propped there against the rough stones he said, "Hud?" in a gruff whisper, and then louder, "Hud, come." A terrible silence settled over him.

"Ah, shit," Jack breathed, lying down again. He felt that primitive urge to wail come back with the horror rising in his chest, but he resisted this time. It hadn't done any good. Even the dog—ah, jeez, his dog, his last hope—had given him up for dead. But he wasn't dead! The dark was pressing in on him; Jack patted and stroked an arm. "It'll be all right," he kept repeating to himself, struggling to still his trembling. He watched the pattern of stars appear through the entrance hole and strained to hear, but that son-of-a-bitch, low-down, no-account mutt really had abandoned him.

That's when Jack started seeing the figures, glimpsed out of the corner of his eye. They flitted, hazy shapes of boys and men, as if thrown by firelight against the stone walls of the *kiva*. At first Jack kept closing his eyes and trying not to acknowledge them, but as the long night wore on he decided to make the best of it—at least he had an audience.

So Jack whispered a story, his favorite story, starting at the beginning as his father crept up through the brush, how he dropped, belly flat, on the rocks and peered through the low branches at the men around the campfire. Some the boy recognized—they were cowhands employed by the Hashknife company. But what were they doing, squatting on their heels with this gang of rustlers?

They kept passing a bottle and the talk got louder, until the boy heard what they were celebrating and how they planned to take the evening's prize catch to the maverick factory on the edge of the Hashknife ranch. They were already set to ship out a trainload of stolen cattle the next morning; now they had Grandpa Jack's big longhorn bull along for bragging rights.

It was the bull Jack's father had been tracking since late afternoon, a big assignment for a twelve-year-old, and he'd taken it seriously. He'd considered going back for help when he saw the confusion of shallow horse prints around the bull's deep funnel tracks, but he'd been drawn on by a youthful curiosity. What sort of men would be so brazen as to steal this lumbering, horn-spanned giant that his father took such pride in?

Now that he'd seen them the boy was already scooting backwards in the dirt, thinking to high-tail it back to his father, joyful—the old man would think him a real hero! But the next moment Jack's dad had been grabbed by the back of his shirt and hoisted up. Now it was the rustlers who were tipping their hats back and looking at him.

"Whooie, would ya lookie here what I caught!" the rustler crowed in Jack's ear. "You all think this here's a spy?"

Both of Jack's feet were off the ground. He twisted in the man's grip, swinging his arms and kicking his legs, then he went limp and the cowboy dropped him. "I'm no spy," the boy said from his knees. He was shivering with fear but his brain was still working: "I come to join up with ya," he announced. "I've runned away."

The company of men laughed but a few stepped out of the circle of firelight to look down at him with murderous eyes. The boy crouching in their midst didn't know it, but in a matter of weeks, Burt Mossman would be hired on as superintendent of the Hashknife outfit, and his first day on the job he would capture three of these men to put on trial as cattle thieves; the rest he would fire and so earn his reputation as the man who tamed the Hashknife. These were the men who prodded young Jack with the toes of their boots and asked him questions that the boy answered breathlessly, lying with such innocent ease that they took him at his word.

Flattop Frank was the one he was given over to then and who Jack's dad was huddled next to, a plate of beans in his hands, when Jack's grandpa and six men from the J Bar bore their horses down into the camp at a dead run. Shots were fired before the dust cleared; the men scattered in a panic.

The boy was face down in the dirt, hands over his ears, when someone tripped over his legs and scrambled back up, cursing. Jack peeked over his shoulder and saw Flattop Frank take a bullet in his chest seconds before the boy registered the gun's report. Frank clawed at the wound, his eyes showing surprise, and the boy screamed and tried to roll out of the way as he dropped.

Still he got pinned beneath the body, the breath knocked out of him, and Jack struggled to push the dying man off but he was so heavy, much heavier than the boy would have thought. Jack's back was soon slick with the dead man's blood, and that's how he slid out from under the body, pulling himself with his hands closer to the fire.

His father was in the circle of light thrown by the campfire, too, and he glanced at Jack before methodically reloading, then sighting down his rifle barrel and firing. One of the J Bar horses was gut-shot by returned fire, and Jack watched his father reel around. "Get away from those horses!" he ordered his men over the animal's anguished squeals. But the other men from the ranch were scared, trying to take cover and shooting wild from over their saddles, still holding onto the reins with one hand and praying for a quick retreat.

Grandpa Jack, on the other hand, was of a mind to finish this thievery once and for all. The ground was littered with bodies as far as the firelight allowed the boy to see. Some were still moving, trying to drag a leg or belly wound off into the cover of brush. Grandpa Jack reloaded his rifle and waited until he was fired upon again so he could turn toward the sound and find his next target.

Finally, one of those rustlers hiding behind a juniper got his breath back and steadied his hand against the rough bark. He drew a true bead on Grandpa Jack's face and blew the whole top his head off.

The boy watched his father twirl, slinging blood and brains, and drop in one fluid motion. Jack crawled closer—"Let's get the hell out of here!" he heard the men from the J Bar saying—and he reached out with one hand but he couldn't make himself touch his father's pants leg.

He was staring at the inches of ground between his fingers and the heavy wool pants his father always wore when somebody pulled him up by the waist and slung him into a saddle. The gut-shot horse took the final bullet, and someone got a rope around the neck of the longhorn bull. Then they were riding home with just one body—his father's—draped over a saddle, their ears ringing in the silence.

Jack moaned as he dreamed, jarred by the horse's motion. The boy would make it home sometime deep in the night; it had fallen to him to wake his mother and younger brothers, to stand beside his mother at the kitchen table as the body was carried in, then to lift the corpse's arms and legs so his ma could wash it, weeping soundlessly, then dress it in Grandpa Jack's good suit. The man's face was gone; they covered it with a towel so as not to frighten the youngest boys when they brought the body out to the parlor.

Some folks would say that Grandpa Jack's wife, Grace, lost her mind that night. She did lock all the doors, refusing the neighbor's offerings of food and condolences and sending away the minister when he arrived on his buggy the next morning. She sat a day-long, lonely, stony vigil by the corpse until the ranch foreman broke out a window, releasing a cloud of flies, and got his men to help him slide the body into its coffin. There wasn't any church ceremony; they'd prepared a grave on a low hill behind the house, and Jack's dad—the man of the house now—read a passage from the Bible while the family and about a dozen ranch hands looked on.

They damn near buried the dead man's dream with him that day. The boy knew his father had seen a paradise in this new land, but what Jack's dad and his mother and four brothers lived through after that was a lot closer to hell.

The drought went on and on, until even the springs that fed into Jack's Canyon dried up. There was little left for the cattle to forage on when this teenage boy made the decision to sell most of their stock at record low prices and pay off his father's debts. Then the blizzard of 1901 blew the Hashknife off the face of the planet, and the J Bar looked likely to follow, its bunkhouse and corrals nearly empty, that white blanket hugging the forms of the land like its shroud.

But, somehow, as a family, they clung to it. Every morning Jack's grandmother Grace put bacon gravy and biscuits on the table, then she and her boys bundled up and went out to tend to their small herd. Jack had heard stories about his grandmother all his life: she could brand, worm, cut horns, and fix fences; she sure as hell saddled her own horse. That's probably why folks in those days thought her crazy. It must have seemed like Grace Rawlings really didn't need a man.

But Jack knew she did. She needed Jack's dad and her other boys to give all the work a reason. And nature, for once, cooperated; maybe the grass never grew 18 inches high again, but sometime in the early 1900's, the J Bar ranch had started looking a little bit more like the paradise Grandpa Jack had died for. Like Jack himself had been willing to die for.

When Jack opened his eyes, a gray light had reentered the *kiva*, and he rose up on his elbows, groaning. Jack was in a sweat by the time he'd sat up and worked his back to the wall; the broken leg had swollen tight inside the fabric of his jeans.

But when he did rest against the stones and raise his head, Jack noticed the spider right away; it was huge, caught in a wedge of light on the western wall of the *kiva*. As he watched, the spider crawled into a crack between the rocks and disappeared, then, miraculously, just as it reemerged—the little bug was looking right at him, he was certain—Jack heard music.

The notes drifted in through the entrance hole, riding on the light, a melodious fluting, coming nearer, up the canyon. Jack was soothed by it at first and closed his eyes to listen better—not a flute, but a harmony of bells. Then he was gasping for breath as he struggled to sit upright. Bells—yes—sheep bells!

"Help," he whispered hoarsely, "help me!" He tried to stand and crumpled, instead, onto the dirt floor of the *kiva*. So he dragged himself over to the dim circle of light and raised his eyes.

There was Hud's black nose, then the dog was digging furiously in the mud roof, sending a rain of dirt down on Jack's head and shoulders. The dog stopped to lower his muzzle into the darkness of the *kiva*, and when he saw Jack he yipped joyfully.

Then, once again, he disappeared. Jack lowered his head until his nose nearly touched the ground, thinking his deliverer had abandoned him. But several heartbeats later Hud was back, frantically digging, filling the air with dust. When Jack heard the echo of the horse's canter, his face split into a wide grin. "Well, I'll be damned," he wheezed at the dirt. "But not yet."

THIRTY-EIGHT

The delivery room nurse was named Angela, and I smiled at her when she told me because I thought it was such an appropriate name for a woman whose job was bringing babies out into the light. She even looked a little angelic; her curly blond hair was pulled back from a full face and her skin was very pale. "My shift's over at 6 a.m.," she said with a wink. "Let's see if you can make a deadline." She stayed with me until Richard got back from the car with my suitcase, then she left us to find some extra pillows while he set up the tape player and dug through my overnight bag to find the Mozart tapes.

I could tell right away when the Pitocin the doctor had ordered for me kicked in; the contractions were now a full minute long and only 2 or 3 minutes apart. Angela gave me my options for pain medication like she was reading from a menu; she made it sound like an epidural was the soup de jour, but I said no to that one. Richard and I had talked about it, and I was more fearful of what I couldn't feel than what I could. So I opted for the intravenous narcotic with the fancy name—unlike Richard, I *had* read the last chapters in our books at home, and that drug's effects were the only things on those pages that had sounded the least bit fun. Besides, we were both exhausted, and as Angela injected the drug into the IV taped to the back of my hand she said, "Okay, honey. This'll help you get some rest."

Then I was floating near the ceiling for a while, returning to my bed every few minutes to breathe through a contraction. Richard shook my arm; he'd bought a couple sandwiches from the hospital cafeteria for our supper, and he told me while we ate that he'd finally spoken to Fred—the girl had finally answered the house phone—but no one had heard from Jack.

Throughout the night there was more Pitocin and more of that narcotic—I was grateful Angela didn't make me ask for it because I felt guilty about floating around so much, but, on the other hand, I really loved that drug. I also loved her and Richard and my father and *Tío* Fred and the nurses' aide who dropped by every twenty minutes or so.

Sometime during the night Richard lowered one of the rails and crawled into bed beside me. Mozart took a break while he slept, and I laid flat on my back like a corpse with my hands pressed together on my big-as-it-was-going-to-get belly. That's when it hit me: I could pray. I said the Our Father very slowly, thoughtfully, but not for me—for my father. I stopped to breathe through another contraction, then I said the Hail Mary that Fred had taught me for my child.

To pass the time I told myself a story, a love story, about a man who was not really young anymore but still handsome, who had suffered and done wrong things but who had thought hard about the evil deeds and the suffering until he'd made himself into a person he could live with. Richard was snoring softly, so I was the one who had to stop to breathe through the pain, counting slowly: one—oh, Jesus, don't clench, just breathe—two . . . three . . . four . . . five. Then I told myself about a woman who was also past her youth and learning how to stop being someone else's child, and finding out how hard it was to grow up and be the one who's responsible for who she was—and who now was going to be someone who was responsible for a helpless little baby, as well.

One . . . two . . . . Oh, God. Oh, God. Three . . . four . . . five. I started at the beginning—how they nearly collided in the doorway of a Walgreens and how, like orbiting electrons, they were already forming a chemical bond. How Sharon was the scientist who eventually combined them into a booth and added coffee, and how the experiment was a success because a week later their eyes kept locking over their dinners and when their knees touched under the table a current passed between them that changed the woman's breathing and made her palms sweat. The man felt it, too, because they stayed connected there, hidden by a tablecloth, long after he'd finished eating and even stopped talking while he gripped the edge of the table and stared at the endive and pieces of gristle left on his plate. One . . . . Shit, I can't do this! Two . . . three . . . four . . . five.

The woman ran when the waitress dropped off their bill, but the man caught up with her in the parking lot, and when he took her hand the tingle traveled through her fingers and all the way up her arm. So the woman invited the man to come to her home sometime for dinner, mostly because she was afraid this feeling was too good to be real. And she knew if that was the case, if the man was false, she could trust her father to sniff that out and tell her the truth. One . . . two . . . three . . . . Argh. Oh, my God. Four . . . five. Her father was crass, he was honest to the point of brutality, but he loved her, she knew, and he would never let anyone harm her.

Their lives were never the same after that. The man came, not just for one dinner, but for many dinners. They'd sit at the kitchen table and talk on and on over their coffee. He was a lot better educated than she was, but the woman was an avid reader and had picked up the strategies of debate from listening to her father, who won every argument by never conceding a point unless it formed the basis of a stronger refutation.

One . . . two . . . . Richard stirred and mumbled the "three . . . four . . . five." They met at the man's apartment, too. For a while they would huddle over her father's checkbook and mismanaged ledgers, then the man would move a stack of books and papers off the couch and they'd sit close together until a silence came over both of them and the woman finally closed her eyes and allowed the man to kiss her.

One day the man broke off their embrace and confessed to her that he had loved a woman who'd died in a car accident, on her way up to Flagstaff to visit him. He'd started crying as he told her how he'd blamed himself and had taken up swimming again, doing thirty minute laps in the university pool at least twice a day, sometimes three or four times a day, because he was afraid he would kill himself if he didn't stop thinking about it—one . . . . God, I am *so* done with this. Two . . . three .

. . four . . . five—and he didn't want to become an alcoholic or drive his own car into a tree. Sweet Jesus. Man. How do people do this?

Okay; keep going. So later, when the woman took him by the hand and led him into his bedroom, she was thinking of comforting him. But it was the woman who found comfort in the swimmer's lean torso and muscular arms. Naked, clinging to him, she dove deeper than she'd ever gone and only surfaced to gulp enough air so she could sink again.

Her father never once reached for his shotgun. Surprising her with his restraint, he offered only glum resistance to the man's increasing presence in her life. When they told him of their plans to marry—over an elaborate seafood gumbo the woman had worked all day on—her father put his fork down and stopped even pretending to eat. One . . . two . . . three . . . four . . . five. That one wasn't so bad. Finally the "gorilla" and "peace-nick" comments ceased, and the girl accepted her father's silence as her release.

She was free to marry; she was free to bear a child. She had ceased to be her father's burden, a reminder of his loss, and her life was now a love story, not a tragedy, anymore.

THIRTY-NINE

Midnight was so black I couldn't see him but the banging stopped the moment I stepped into the barn and then I heard him huff like he was saying, "Who the hell are you?" or maybe, "Finally—someone to let me out of here!" which was exactly what I intended to do. I figured just following the road toward the lights of Winslow would get Midnight and me back to town, and I could probably find my way to the group home and then keep him in the stable there for the night. Because I wasn't going to steal him, I swear.

I'd seen where Fred kept the bridles and had grabbed one on my way in, feeling along the wall until I touched leather and heard the jingle of a bit. Then I had my hand on the latch of Midnight's stall, the smell of the horse in my nose, and I was tempted—so f-ing tempted—to go for the rush, the launch into that impossible future again, where I could feel the wind and the earth rushing under me and never stop, just keep on going, right off the edge of things and into a thoughtless void.

"*Niña?*" Fred had said behind me. That's all he'd said: "girl." But there was a question in it, and I knew what the question was.

I must have seemed guilty as hell the way I whirled around, standing there with a bridle in hand. "He . . . he's lonely," I stammered. I think I even tried to hide the damn bridle behind my back. Stupid shit.

Fred had a flashlight in his good hand, pointed down at the straw at our feet. He raised it a little to point with its light back to the barn door. "I made up one of the other bunks for you. You can stay with me, *niña.*" He was already turning, following the beam of his flashlight. "*No me gustan los fantasmas tampoco,*" he muttered.

I could still do it, leap onto that horse, rush the old guy out of my way, and go. I imagined Fred gimp-walking in a big hurry up to the house—it'd take him forever just to get to a phone, and I'd be long gone. But I didn't. I followed him out. I even hung that bridle up on its empty nail.

Because here was the question in that one word: was I going to really stop being Rose and go on being Jane, the girl with no history but the promise of a future, who might someday have a real home and people who loved her and trusted her? Or was I doomed to always being crazy Rose, the one no one wanted, would ever want, the lost girl who no one would ever even try to find?

FORTY

Changing Woman stood outside her dwelling looking sad as she watched Sun's passage across the sky. She had once rejoiced in his warmth but now he seemed so distant; he had drawn away from her, and now their son had, too. For days at a time Monster Slayer traveled the mesas and mountains seeking to abate his blood lust. But Changing Woman knew blood would always cry out for more blood. She lowered her gaze to earth and wept.

It might be that it was Changing Woman's tears that called down the storm that began gathering that same afternoon. Thick clouds rolled in from the south and were met by thunderheads from the north; lightning arched overhead followed by the bellow of thunder. Sitting by her fire, Changing Woman felt the hairs stand up on the back of her neck. The next instant her son stood, drenched, in her doorway. He said nothing but stripped off his armor and dumped his weapons and latest trophy in a pile. He sat beside her as she ladled his meal into a bowl.

All that night it rained and the winds howled around their *hogan*. All the next day the clouds blocked out the sun and hail poured from the sky. Their only light was their cooking fire and the flashes of lightning; thunder shook dirt from the roof onto their heads. They huddled together for four days and four nights, then on the fifth day, the sky cleared.

When Changing Woman and Monster Slayer ventured from their house they could not believe their eyes. Trees lay scattered about and boulders had tumbled over one another in their hurry to wash down from the mountains. "Nature has saved us!" Changing Woman exclaimed. "Our dwelling was spared, that is a great blessing, but we live safely on a plain. Those monsters who were left—the ones you had yet to find and kill—they live in the mountains. Surely they were smashed to bits in all this weather!"

Monster Slayer was gazing about in disbelief at all the destruction. No man could ever have caused such damage: grass and soil crevassed into canyons, streams turned into roaring rivers boiling with rocks.

"It's certain that all the *Naayéé'* are gone now," repeated Changing Woman. "You need never go chasing monsters again."

FORTY-ONE

A Navajo man's broad, brown face appeared through the gaping roof of the *kiva*. "Holy shit," he said, pushing the dog aside with one hand, "You all right, grandpa?"

"Please," Jack said softly, lifting an arm, "get me out of here."

"Yeah, sure," the man said, but then they both heard the crack of timbers giving way beneath him and the man had to scramble back, off the roof. "Jeez. Hold on. Just a minute." Jack heard the man's voice and footsteps receding but Hud came back and was grinning down at him when the footsteps returned. "Go on, now," the voice said to the dog, then a hand dangled an old metal canteen with a worn, fabric cover into the hole by its strap.

When it plunked down at Jack's side with a heavy, sloshing sound, Jack pulled the canteen toward him and fumbled off the metal cap. He raised himself up on one elbow and poured water into his parched throat, letting it run down both sides of his mouth, then he wiped the water, moaning, around his grizzled cheeks and forehead with the back of his hand. Jack took another big gulp of water and jammed the cap back on the canteen before he sighed, "Thank you," in a barely audible whisper. A cloth bundle dropped beside him in the circle of light.

"There's some bread and stuff in there," the voice said. "How long you been here?"

"Two nights," Jack replied hoarsely. "You got to get me out. I got a busted leg, fallin' in." Then he was dizzy from the effort of speaking.

The man risked leaning forward, shading his eyes with his hat, to peer down at him. "I better go for help."

"No! God, no," Jack squeaked out. "Don't go."

But the man had inched backwards from the edge again. "I'll be back soon's I can. This here's your dog, ain't it? You stay here, boy," Jack heard the man tell Hud. "He's a damn fine dog," the man added in a louder voice. "He showed up at my grandma's *hogan* last night. She figured he'd come to tell her something. And he brought me right out here."

"You got a horse, right?" Jack asked, interrupting him. "Just toss a rope down."

"Yeah, I got a horse, but I don't have any rope. I'll get one, though."

The man's voice was getting fainter; he was going away, and it made Jack desperate. "Wait," he cried weakly. But he could hear the horse snorting now, hooves turning on the ground overhead.

"I'll send my wife into town for some help and come right back," the voice assured him.

"Wait," Jack said again, but the horse was cantering off. He slumped over the canteen and rested his cheek against its wool fabric, sick with disappointment. At the same time, Hud let out a loud sigh and rested his head on his paws. "Well, how the hell do you think I feel?" Jack whispered up at him.

Jack finally remembered the cloth bundle and clumsily unwrapped the man's fry bread, dried peaches and cheese. At first Jack didn't even think he was hungry, but by the second or third bite he was ravenous, and he lay there picking crumbs off the cloth long after he'd chewed down the rest of the man's lunch.

But then Jack didn't feel very well at all. He pillowed his cheek on the hard metal canteen and gazed, one-eyed, up at the panting dog. "You are a good mutt," Jack told him grudgingly. "I won't say I'm wastin' money when I pay for your shots anymore." Hud was indifferent to the praise; he got up, pelting Jack with pebbles and dirt, and left him to find some shade.

Jack's stomach churned and clenched, and he started moaning and groaning and generally making a much bigger fuss than he had the rest of the time he'd been down in the *kiva*. The flies had returned with the heat, but Jack barely had the strength to wave them away. And the smell of the dead snake seemed to grow more noxious every minute.

What if the man didn't come back? In fact, why the hell would he? Jack wasn't kin to him. He probably had plenty of other things to do besides figuring out how to pull a half dead white guy out of a hole.

Then the chills started up again and Jack laid on the bench shaking and dreaming with his eyes wide open, staring into the ragged blue circle over his head, and there were sheets flapping in the wind, a long line of them, blinding white in the sun. Jack's mother, Elizabeth, was there, complaining about those sheets, blaming them for the cataracts in both of her eyes. It scared Jack a little; he knew the woman was long dead.

"If your pa'd a done right by me from the start instead of cow-towing to *his* ma like he did, I might have seen my own way to the grave. He let her run him, right up to the day she died. All her boys did. The old woman hated outsiders, and nobody whose name weren't Rawlings or hadn't signed on with them could even set foot on that ranch without somebody pointin' a shotgun at 'em.

"She knew who I was, though. I made sure she knew who I was. Grace Rawlings would come into town every Sunday, as if she really were a Christian woman, and I'd be there at the church. I would endure all that hissing behind my back so's I could sit in the same pew as her and exhale my breath into her damn air and leaf through that hymnal she knew she was going to have to touch some day. Like she knew her son—your pa—was touchin' me. Polite like—we weren't married yet—but still . . . .

"It's 'cause of her I burned out my eyes, helpin' to pay for my keep, washing all those sheets at that damn railroad hotel and stringing them up in the face of that hard sun. And you may as well know that others spoke poorly of me for waitin' on your dad like that, but he wouldn't marry, and he sure as hell wouldn't take me home, until the old lady gave her say so.

"My people were good folk, not rich or nothin', but decent. We had a nice little dairy farm in a backwater town in east Kansas, and if I'd a had any sense, I would've stayed put. But then I visited the first Harvey House there in Topeka and got a notion to come west—hell's bells, I was just a girl, all of eighteen. What did I know about life, about men and their mothers, anyway?

"So I answered Fred Harvey's newspaper ad. And I was just as good a 'biscuit shooter' as any of 'em, just ask your pa. He come out to the La Posada every day of the week after I got there. It weren't even a month 'afor he'd asked me to wait for him.

"I washed them damn sheets and hung 'em out, I scrubbed floors and made a hundred beds. Because I thought, if I could just bide my time, the old woman would relent. Well, she died, instead, right in the middle of the Great War. Do ya think I was sad? She did it to herself; she plum wore herself out, workin' harder than any man for so many years.

"Afterwards your pa burned their old farmhouse down to the ground. It was the only way he could really be rid of the old woman. Then he built us a fine home and tried to be a good husband, even though his own brothers could barely speak a civil word to me, and I dare say, they were more'n a little jealous. None of the other boys ever did marry, Jack—now you tell me their mother wasn't at fault in that!

"Maybe I was a little lonely at first, even with all them wranglers and critters around, but after a while I really didn't mind being out there on the ranch all by ourselves. Them was good years for raisin' cattle, and we was all plenty busy.

"But then all those curses I'd hung up with the boarding house sheets started coming back at me, only now they were my sheets, skinned off the bed and burned because I could never get that blood out. I did carry one child full term before you, Jack—a little girl—but she come out with the cord wrapped like a noose around her neck.

"I figured I was done with my penance when you came along, and then George. Don't close your eyes, Jack—I want you to listen to this. The Great Depression was a hard, hard time, but our debts were paid and we were hanging on. Banks failed, but so what? They weren't carrying our note. Beef prices hit bottom, but our cattle weren't starving and neither were we. I thought for years that the world could go ahead and change but that it wouldn't necessarily apply to me and mine. Then in '32 my son died, and of a sudden, it wasn't just other peoples' bad luck anymore.

"They had to pry little Georgie out of my arms—do you remember? You hated that hospital and I didn't blame ya—they wouldn't let you near your little brother until he was limp in my arms and you watched them doctors and nurses tear him away from me.

"Here now—you listen. What difference does it make if a bull's got horns wider than a man's out-stretched arms? There ain't much you can do with a bull in your arms, now is there? The thing you're going to want one more time in your lap is your own little boy, the one whose lungs have filled up with water, or the one who's run off and sits in the company of the most dangerous men in the territory, or the little girl who's afraid all her life you never loved her.

"It won't be the ranch you'll turn in your grave with longing for. It won't be them cows that keeps our blood alive long after your veins are running dust."

Jack wanted to acknowledge his mother's words in some way but he was drifting, skating like those clouds across a vast blue sky. He started hearing the voices of other ghosts, Chinese men speaking somewhere nearby, and then he realized he was in his grave and they were shoveling the dirt in on top of him. He could barely open his eyes when he felt someone drop onto the floor beside him and lift his arm.

"Hang on, grandpa," he heard one of the voices say. "We're going to get you out of here."

Jack believed in the resurrection. He felt the angel hovering over him, then he tried to swallow as his head was lifted and water rushed past his cracked lips. He could hear low groans under the strange

Mongolian words as hands lifted his shoulders. A bolt of pain shot up his leg and something was fastened to his back—his wings, no doubt.

Then he was rising, on a jerky, swaying flight amid shouts of caution—"Okay, keep it steady. Watch his head! Okay. Steady now. Go ahead. You've almost got it." Jack felt the light on his face and tried to open his eyes again but was blinded by its glory. More voices clamored around him, jubilant cries, words of astonishment, then he was jolted down and the straps that had bound him were released.

The angels gathered around him. Jack felt their shade and peeked cautiously. A Navajo woman returned his smile. "You're going to be all right," she assured him. Jack felt pressure on his arm, a prick on the back of one hand, then fingers opened his eyelid and a pin of light searched inside.

"I'm alive," Jack whispered to the woman, and she nodded, her smile widening, yes. "And my dog, where's my . . . .?"

"He's right here. He's fine. We're gonna get you to the clinic in Ganado," she told him as his stretcher was lifted again.

Now Jack could see the crowd he had gathered. "Hey. Take it easy," one of the attendants told him, but Jack struggled to rise on his elbows. A fire engine was parked beside the ruin, pickup trucks and police vehicles lined the dirt road. A crowd of people still stood around the *kiva*, talking, pulling in ropes and shaking their heads in amazement.

When they loaded his stretcher into the back of the ambulance, Jack sat up all the way. He waved and a young woman, standing to one side, holding a horse by the reins, saw him. She pointed and laughed. Then everyone was turning toward him, smiling, waving back, as the doors were closed and the ambulance wailed on its way.

FORTY-TWO

I was working harder than I ever have in my life. This was why it was called "labor," I realized as the sweat poured down my face. A few minutes earlier the pain had been so bad that I was ready to quit, to call the whole thing off, but now I was too busy to be bothered by something as measly as pain. Richard's job was lifting my shoulders up off the bed so I could bear down with each contraction, and he was imitating Angela or some swimming coach he used to have: "You can do it—push! Push! Come on, honey, push! Okay, good job. You're doing fine. Rest a minute. Just rest, okay. Now? Okay, here we go. Now, push! Come on, push hard! Push hard, hard, hard! That's it, that's it. Great job, honey. Okay, it's okay, you can relax."

By the time the doctor came around we were an expert team, and he stood there, smiling, while he watched us, then he pulled up a stool and disappeared behind my knees. He told us the baby's head was crowning but it kept pulling back between contractions. That didn't worry me; I was in control again, and the baby's heartbeats were beeping through the monitor at a steady, purposeful rate.

Richard lifted; I pushed. We rested and started again. "His head is turned to the side," the doctor told us. "You're going to have to bear down really hard." Then Richard's face blanched a pasty white as the doctor made the incision for the episiotomy. Angela took his elbow and asked him if he was okay. They didn't seem worried about me, although that was *my* blood I could see all over the end of the bed. And that was fine; I was too busy for idle chit-chat—and besides, pain is a relative thing.

That helped; the baby's head and then a shoulder were out. I caught a glimpse of Angela's face behind my knees and she was glowing, really happy. "Here comes the baby," the doctor said. "Sit up and look—you can see it!" Richard had an awed look on his face, gazing down at our child, but I shouted, "No! Just get it the hell out of me!"

Then it was out, and Richard kissed me with tears in his eyes. "It's a perfect little girl," the doctor crowed, and I cried, too, I was so happy.

Angela brought me our daughter and urged me to offer her my breast. Yes, our baby girl had ten fingers and ten toes. She was beautiful, with a full mane of Richard's black hair, red-faced, pointy-headed and squish-nosed. Best of all, she was alive and, more than ever, so was I.

FORTY-THREE

Tío Fred shook me awake the next morning before it was really even light; he'd already scrambled us some eggs and wrapped them in tortillas. I ate with the scratchy blanket still wrapped around me on the bunk while he plotted out our day: I was to fill all the water troughs and measure out the hay and coffee can of oats to all the horses, then we were going to get Midnight into one of the back corrals, somehow—he seemed a little vague about that—then I was going to get my first driving lesson. Apparently there was some old truck in the machine shed he thought would get us to town for groceries and a stop at the hospital. Like I said, some people are *way* too trusting, but I was so jazzed by the thought of learning how to drive that even the prospect of killing poor old Fred—not to mention myself—maneuvering clutch and gas on an old stick shift wasn't going to deter me.

We both turned at the distant tinkling sound of the phone ringing up at the house, and by the time *Tío* Fred gestured I was already up and running out the door. Mr. C.'s voice on the phone seemed so high-pitched it was nearly unrecognizable, but "It's a girl! A beautiful girl. Six pounds, one once," finally sunk in on me, and by then Fred was coming in the screen door with his hand out for the receiver. I used the bathroom and when I came out Fred was grinning like crazy—you could tell the old man really loved Mr. C. and his wife, and he kept talking about them the whole time he was following me around while I did my chores. He said he'd practically raised Katrina and that she'd always called him "*tío*," uncle, and that I should, too. Then he told me he'd come to this place when he was 16, a runaway, and that a man he called *Señor* Rawlings had taken him in and put him to work.

That's when it hit me. I kept my head down, kinda, not really letting on, but while I wrestled that halter over Midnight's sharp, black ears and then led him slowly toward the opened corral, one hand on the throat latch, the other on the halter rope right below the tie line, with Fred on the other side gripping mane with his good hand and cooing at him in Spanish, it was really sinking in. *Tío* Fred *needed* me, and Mr. C. had just had a baby—*he* needed me. Maybe even Mrs. C. and that little girl might need me. I wouldn't mind holding a baby. And they might actually *let* me.

I cried while we stood there watching Midnight race the circuit of that corral, hoping *Tío* Fred wouldn't notice because of all the dust. It was a beautiful sight, that black beast, head high, tail flying, thundering past us. Then the stallion skidded to a stop, reared back, and pawed the air. I let *Tío* Fred pat my back, then, and wiped at my nose. I just couldn't stop bawling, I was so happy.

ENEMY BLESSINGS

When Monster Slayer's mother had said, "Now you can stop visiting those monsters' dwellings and remain here with me," he had felt only frustration, not relief. So the next day when Wind sought him out and whispered to him, Monster Slayer bent his head and listened with great attention. Wind said not all of the monsters that plagued human lives were dead, and he told Monster Slayer about Old Age Woman, one of the few who yet remained. She seemed bent and weak but knew how to drain one's power so slowly, hour by hour, day by day, week by week, month by month, year by year, all unnoticed until every bit of strength was sapped.

Monster Slayer hurried to where he had left his weapons. When he saw Changing Woman watching him with alarm he said: "I know from Wind that at least one survives." When she put one hand on her hip he added quickly: "I wish to be certain the People are truly safe."

Changing Woman shook her head at her son. "Don't you realize that some of our enemies should remain?"

Monster Slayer felt his chest swell again with the pride of his many victories. "You do not need to worry about me or help me, Mother. I have set out to destroy our enemies. That is what I intend to do." And since Wind had also told Monster Slayer he could find The One Who Brings Old Age where the sheep gather on the mountain, the young man set off at once.

It was a long journey but eventually Monster Slayer came upon a white-haired, wrinkled old woman, hobbling along with her boney back bent over her cane. "Hello, old grandmother," he said to her. "You are meeting now the man who is going to kill you."

The old woman stopped. She scuffed around to face him and slowly tilted her head to peer up at him with her rheumy eyes. She smiled, showing her few remaining, worn out teeth. "Why would you kill me?" she rasped in her old woman voice. "I have not harmed you. I am just a weak, old woman."

"You lie!" Monster Slayer shouted over her words. "You will devour my people just as the Alien Monsters would have done if I had not killed them!"

The old woman's smile broadened. "So you are Monster Slayer," she told him mildly. "I have heard of your brave efforts to help your people. But you should not kill me." And with that, the old woman resumed her deliberate movement down the trail.

Monster Slayer was infuriated. He stomped after her, saying, "I have set out to destroy my people's enemies. That is what I intend to do."

The old woman stopped but she did not turn around. Instead she asked him over the hump of her back and the knob of her shoulder: "And how will you save your people from themselves? Once they realize there is no one slowly stealing their strength, why will they suffer all the woes of raising children? And then who will care for all these worthless old people who are living on and on? Your people need me. I inspire them to care for their babies so they can pass their wisdom on." The old woman turned her face back to the path. She hesitated, then straightened ever-so-slightly, planted her cane, and continued tottering away.

Monster Slayer followed her only with his eyes. This time the defender of the Diné would return to his mother empty-handed.

* * * * *

Monster Slayer had no sooner returned home when Wind spoke to him again: "The monster who freezes the water your people need to drink, scatters their prey, rips the leaves from the trees, and shivers your corns fields still walks the earth. Will you not defend your people from Cold Woman?"

So Monster Slayer asked his mother to tell him where he could find Cold Woman and slay her. But Changing Woman put both of her hands on her hips this time and said: "My son, you are very brave, but it seems you are still learning. There are some things that people should not try to change."

"Never mind," Monster Slayer responded. He was already strapping on his battle sandals. "I know where the snow never melts. That is where she'd dwell."

So he climbed to the highest part of the mountain, stumbling over the boulders just below its peak to where the wind and cold had turned trees into twisted, stunted stumps. There he found patches of snow and a skinny, old woman sitting on the icy ground, naked and shivering.

"Grandmother, now you are meeting Monster Slayer, the man who will end your life!" he announced.

"Good," she answered through chattering teeth. "I have had enough of this miserable existence. But you should know this: when I am gone your people will sweat every day of the year. The snow will no longer replenish the Earth and give it time to rest. The streams will slow to trickles and then disappear entirely. As will your people, over time." The old woman blew on her hands and rubbed them together, then wrapped both arms around her skinny, trembling frame.

Monster Slayer was appalled at her words. "I supposed it is better that I don't kill you, after all," he said. He lowered his hand and his eyes. Once again the defender of the Diné returned to his mother without a trophy.

* * * * *

Wind came whistling down the canyons and into the home of Monster Slayer just moments after he had crossed its threshold. "Defender of the *Diné*, here you are, returning to your mother when there are monsters still afoot. Do you know of these Poverty Creatures who live in the buttes? They use everything up—tools and blankets, cooking pots, clothes. Your people will soon be destroyed by them!"

Monster Slayer sighed. These monsters sounded dreadful, indeed. But Changing Woman was making a meal to celebrate his return. She wouldn't be pleased if he just turned around and left again. "Mother, surely you know where these creatures live."

"Eat and rest," Changing Woman answered. "We'll talk later." She wouldn't even raise her eyes from the food she was preparing to look at him, but she said quietly down at her mutton stew: "Some things are best left the way they are."

"I have promised to destroy my people's enemies," he said. "I guess I will have to find them myself in the buttes."

So he traveled there and climbed to the top of the mesa. From there he could see the sacred mountains anchoring the earth in each direction. He also saw a shack of a dwelling on the edge of the cliff. Monster Slayer walked over and peered inside. He saw a raggedy old man and an equally dirty old woman sitting on the dirt floor. They had no furniture, no blankets, no pots or pans or bowls or spoons, and absolutely no food.

"Hello Grandfather and Grandmother," Monster Slayer said. "I'm sorry, but this is your last breath. I, Monster Slayer, have come to put an end to you and all the suffering you bring my people."

"What a nice young man," they answered in unison. "You seem to care very deeply about your people. Of course, if that is true, you better change your mind about killing us."

Monster slayer looked around their barren hovel. He did not believe there could be any reason to spare these monsters. But he listened as the old woman said, "People will never change their clothes. They'll wear the same thing, over and over and over . . . ."

"People will never invent better tools," the old man said. "They'll just keep using the same old familiar ones over and over and over . . . ."

"Don't you want your people to think of new ways of sewing and carving and making things?" the old woman asked.

Monster Slayer had no answer for her. He turned away from their terrible poverty and made his way home.

* * * * *

When Wind came whispering around him again, Monster Slayer tried not to listen. But this time Wind told him about Hunger Man who lived on the grassy slope. Monster Slayer did not announce his intentions to his mother this time. He knew exactly what she would say.

Monster Slayer walked a long time and finally saw in the distance twelve amazingly fat creatures ripping plants and trees out of the ground and stuffing them into their chomping mouths as fast as they could. Hunger Man, the biggest, most pot-bellied, and oldest among them was feasting on cactus, popping one after another into the gaping hole in his face and crunching, crunching, crunching away.

"Hunger Man," Monster Slayer shouted. "Do you see me approaching? I am Monster Slayer, here to put an end to you once and for all! For too long my people have suffered from hunger and the threat of starvation."

Hunger Man did not stop chewing and he did not cover his mouth as he mumbled through his next bite of cactus: "I really don't blame you for not liking me. But if you do kill me, you will do more harm than good." Hunger Man reached for more cactus and jammed it in his mouth. "You see," he said through gnashing teeth, "your people need me to inspire them to eat. With me around, they can clearly see the need to plant and harvest crops. They take good care of their livestock because of me. And I am the one who gets the hunter into the woods and causes him to care about how carefully he preserves his game." All this Hunger Man said without ever ceasing to stuff himself.

Monster Slayer knew what Hunger Man said was true. He took no trophy home this time, either.

When Monster Slayer approached his home again he saw Changing Woman was waiting for him by the fire. "So here you are again with nothing to show for all your trouble," she observed. "Maybe you have lost your will to fight the *Naayéé'*."

Monster Slayer sat beside his mother. He took off his sandals and his war shirt. He put his weapons down. "I have come to realize, Mother," he informed her solemnly, "that some things happen for a reason. Perhaps someday you'll understand." Then he stretched out his long legs and sighed, "For now, and for as long as I care to be, I am home."

Changing Woman regarded her son, his arms folded over his chest, eyes already closing, with satisfaction. It made her so happy—he was alive! And for as long as he wished to be, he was home.

FORTY-FIVE

When the phone rang, Jack figured it was another well-wisher calling to see how he was getting along, so he ignored it and let one of the orderlies standing around his bed pick it up while he went on with his story about the greenhorn neighbor who'd turned his entire herd loose in a field full of broom grass and then come charging onto Jack's porch, all red in the face, accusing Jack of poisoning his cattle in order to drive him off his valuable land. Who could blame Jack for pumping a round of buckshot into the idiot's radiator? How else was he going to get the fool's attention long enough to explain a thing or two?

A reporter for the local paper had gotten Jack started by asking about his ordeal in the *kiva*, but once Jack had covered that, he'd felt compelled to go on regaling the young man and the nurses and orderlies who kept dropping by with other tales of his heroic adventures. "Check out this old *Bilagáana*," one native man, leaving, whispered to another, coming in. Jack wasn't at all uncomfortable with this celebrity status; hell, he'd been reborn in a *kiva*—that had to count for *something*.

His leg had been x-rayed, ice-packed to reduce the swelling, and finally set in a plaster cast. Now Jack was back on his pain and stomach medicines, fully hydrated, and feeling his oats again. His leg was hitched up to a complicated pulley system and loomed over his bed like a huge dinosaur bone. It appeared he wouldn't be going anywhere for a while, and he had settled back on his pillows and was running at the mouth to pass the time.

But when the orderly handed him the phone and Jack heard his daughter's voice, all the bluster went right out of him. The girl started off fine, but the next minute she was crying, and she didn't stop when he assured her he was doing great, just a little fracture of the thigh bone, and otherwise great, just great. He couldn't grasp what baby she was talking about until she turned the phone over to Richard and his son-in-law explained it from the beginning.

"I didn't think it was time yet," Jack said defensively. He felt bad; he hadn't intended to run out on the girl.

"Yes," Richard conceded, "she's about three weeks early. A little girl, Jack. Six pounds, one ounce."

"So it's a girl," Jack repeated.

Richard had gone right on explaining some kind of medical problem that was going on, but Jack was busy figuring out if he was disappointed or not. Just because his grandchild was a girl didn't mean she'd *have* to hate cows and horses, did it? He heard Richard say he should keep thinking positive; that's when Jack gathered there was actually something wrong with the kid.

"Kate's pretty upset. They want to keep the baby for treatment and discharge us, and she's refusing to go. I don't know what she thought talking to you would accomplish, but. . . ."

"You tell her I'm on my way," he commanded Richard, then he told the orderly who took the phone from him, "Get me my clothes. And get my god-damned leg down. There's a duffel around here somewheres. I want to see the man who can write up my discharge. Now. The rest of you'll have to excuse me. I've got a new grandchild to see to." Jack was trying to sit up, searching over the sheet for the gadget that moved the bed. "Send me a copy of that story, son. Nurse, call Doc Levy. You tell him to order the ambulance and get me to Winslow General."

Jack grew furious at every attempt to dissuade him, he barked orders at anyone who even passed by his room, and in a matter of hours his insistent demands had gotten him dressed, loaded onto a wheelchair, and rolled to the back door of an ambulance for the ride down to Winslow.

There was a further short delay while they battled over whether the dog, who'd been allowed to loiter in the hospital's driveway, could ride along. Jack was truly torn; he knew his daughter came first, but how could he leave the mutt? Finally the driver admitted that he'd let Hud in the cab on the way from the accident site to the hospital, so maybe one more infraction wouldn't matter. "Let's get on with it, then," Jack snapped, and he gritted his teeth and endured the jostling that got his wheelchair and IV into the vehicle.

Then as they crossed the reservation Jack watched the turkey vultures through the back window of the ambulance. He asked several times why their siren wasn't on but got no satisfactory answer. The damn vultures were wheeling through the dying light, circling in tighter and tighter curves, closing in.

"How much longer?" Jack finally asked the young Navajo man riding in the back of the ambulance with him, because by this time Jack had decided the reason Richard had told him to be positive was that the baby might not live.

The man leaned down to look out the window. "Well, we're about at Wide Ruin Wash. Then it's fifteen miles to the Interstate, another forty to Holbrook, and thirty more to Winslow. You doin' all right?"

"Hell, no, I'm not all right," Jack answered sourly. His leg ached, his bowels were churning, he was dying of cancer, for Christ's sake. But most of all he was ashamed for having gone off on this fool's errand when his daughter and now his grandchild had really needed him.

"Here, let me get you another pillow," the young man offered, crouching under the low ceiling of the ambulance and opening a cupboard. "Then you just try to rest easy and enjoy the scenery."

The man's name—Robert Etsitty—was spelled out on the tag pinned to his blue uniform. "You ever done anything really stupid, Robert?" Jack asked him when the big man had squeezed back down the aisle and returned to his fold-down seat by the rear doors.

Robert laughed and turned away from Jack, watching the vultures riding the thermals over a mesa's steep edge. "You mean like not lookin' where I'm goin' when I decide to take a walk?"

"Hell, you don't know the worst of it," Jack assured him, coming up on his elbows again. "I was on my way to have my own little pow-wow with the Secretary of the Interior, you know. Damn good thing I fell in that hole."

Robert glanced at Jack and shrugged.

"Come to think of it, I must of lost that pistol somewheres."

"I think the Tribal Police picked it up," Robert told him, still gazing out the window. "Maybe you could still get charged with somethin', you know—a firearms violation, or a DWI, or defacing a historic landmark. So maybe, Mr. Rawlings," Robert turned and briefly met Jack's eyes, "you shouldn't talk about it too much."

Jack sighed and lowered his head back against his pillows, then folded his hands on his chest and watched the sky darken past the Navajo man's profile. His thoughts drifted to another evening, a hell of a long time ago now, when he and Fred had been riding home after a tiring day of searching for strays. He'd worked the ridgeline on Maggie, hazing the wayward cattle down the washes toward Fred, who'd driven all the steers, the renegade cows with their calves, into the portable corral with the rest of the herd, then they'd loaded the stock trucks with the help of several other men of their outfit. Now he and Fred were allowing their weary horses to take their time on the way home. There was still work going on back at the ranch, unloading the trucks and sorting the herd into their various corrals, and the boys had been in no hurry.

They both carried their pistols low on their thighs, like gunslingers, in those days, but all they ever shot at were snakes or coyotes, or quail, if they saw them, or doves, sometimes. They seldom hit a thing. That day, from the saddle, he spotted a rabbit—just a little one—stretched out under a bush. He reined in his horse and looked down at it, and while Maggie was shifting her weight from one tired hoof to the next, snorting and playing with the bit, the rabbit rolled onto its back and left its little furry belly exposed.

By this time Fred had circled around, and when Jack had slipped his pistol from its holster and pointed it, Fred had just enough time to say, "No, Jack, don't . . . ." But the report of the gun cut right through his words. He'd swung down from the saddle, lifted the mess of blood and fur by its long ears, and stood grinning up at Fred like an idiot.

Fred had pulled back on his reins, a look of horror on his face. "It's bad luck," he said, crossing himself. "*Esta muy malo—sangre del inocente.*" He'd turned his horse and bolted for home.

"Blood of the innocent," Jack mumbled out loud to the back of Robert's head and the flat, deep blue sky behind him. At the time, he'd thought nothing of the incident. But years later when he'd weighed his dead son in his hands, it came rushing back to him. Fred had been right. There was nothing more terrible. Nothing could haunt you more.

Jack stewed in silence for a long time. He felt the ambulance slow down to turn onto the entrance ramp, then speed up on the freeway. "But Katie didn't do nothin' to deserve it," he said finally. He closed his eyes and clamped his jaw against a growing sense of urgency.

It was dark when they finally reached the city limits, and the hospital's emergency sign cast a red glow over the entrance. The attendant went inside first, and Jack heard the driver open his own door and then the passenger door and speak to the dog. By the time Robert returned with someone to help him get Jack unloaded, he was trying to climb back into his wheelchair on his own. "Hang on, there, now. What's the rush?" the young man asked him, but Jack would not take the time to explain.

"To the counter there. Hurry!" he insisted, even though they were already pushing his chair toward the admitting nurse's station. "Where is my daughter?" Jack demanded, slapping his hand down on the counter. "I want her to know I'm here."

Robert handed the nurse Jack's duffel bag and his paperwork, tapped Jack on the shoulder and said, "Take somebody with you next time you go star-gazin' on the rez, okay?" Then he smiled and wished the nurse good luck as he left.

Jack was talking right over his words. "Katherine Ann Rawlings. My daughter. What room is she in?"

"I can answer your questions in a minute, sir. Right now I need you to fill out this form . . . ."

But the nurse was interrupted by a white-haired, elderly gentleman who said, "Excuse me, ma'am," and pointed. Jack turned to look over his shoulder, and even he was a bit surprised to see a big, black dog in the hospital lobby.

Hud was actually only half inside, standing on the pressure sensitive door pad and scanning the room for Jack. The ambulance attendant stopped to pat his head on his way out but the dog barely glanced at him and didn't even wag his tail. Then Hud lowered his head and dropped to his belly when Jack wheeled all the way around and scowled at him.

"That's my dog," Jack said, glancing back at the nurse. "He's not generally dangerous. I'll make him go on out of here right quick if you'll give me my daughter's room number."

The nurse raised her eyebrows at Jack. "There are no dogs allowed in here, Mister Rawlings. Maybe you can call someone to come get him—a neighbor, perhaps?" But by this time the white-haired man had taken it upon himself to shoo the dog away and was shuffling over to Hud, saying, "Go on now, go on, get away," and pushing the air with his hands.

"I would hate for him to bite that fella," Jack mused loudly. He wished Hud would act a little more ferocious instead of just lying there with his head on his paws. Finally the dog looked up and yawned.

"Sir," the nurse called, trying to get the old man's attention. Then, "Jerry," she said to the orderly who'd helped roll Jack in, "go on over there and chase that dog outside." Jerry, a young black man, sauntered around the counter with his hands crossed on his chest and approached the dog warily.

The nurse sighed loudly and tapped a few keys on her computer. "What was the name again?" Jack rolled back to face her and repeated his daughter's name but she shook her head. "She's been discharged."

Jack was devastated. He had taken too long to get here. "Try the baby's name—Crawford—then," he told her. When the nurse hesitated, he shouted, "Hud, git," without turning around. The dog jumped up and scooted around the corner, his tail curled between his legs.

This time the nurse said, "Okay, yeah. There is a *Grace* Crawford, in the nursery on the second floor. Wait—you're the one I. . . . Hey! Jerry!"

Jack had yanked out the IV needle and was rolling his wheelchair as fast as he could toward a waiting elevator.

"Wait. Don't hurt yourself, Mr. Rawlings," he heard the nurse call after him. "It's all right, Jerry. Just let him go."

Jack did tap his cast against the back wall of the elevator and had to bite down hard against a howl of pain. He twisted around in the chair to punch the "two" button, muttering, "Hold on, girl, I'm comin'. Hold on." But he knew, even before the doors opened and he heard his daughter's voice, that dead or alive, Katie would never leave her child.

"You don't always have to understand me, Richard. You go ahead, if you want to." Jack was backing into the corridor when Kate caught sight of him. She pushed her way past Doc Levy and her husband, her hand coming up to cover her mouth. "Daddy," she said through her fingers and her tears, and Jack was suddenly reminded of her voice as a child. "Oh, thank God you're here."

Jack held out his arms to her. He felt awkward doing it, but the girl rushed to embrace him, and he pulled her head down to kiss her hair and hugged her against his chest. She looked so worn out. "It's all right, now. I'm here now," he assured her gruffly while he patted her back.

Jack squared his shoulders as the two men approached them. He offered Richard his hand and said, "Yeah, yeah," to the younger man's welcome.

"Jack, nobody told me you'd been admitted," Doc Levy said.

"Well, I skipped some of the formalities." Jack found his daughter's hand and squeezed it. "I was in a hurry to see my granddaughter."

Katie straightened up, trying to smile and wiping at her face with one hand while Jack kept a tight grip on the other. "How's she doin'?" he asked her, and he was scared, really scared, until she nodded.

"The last test showed a little improvement. She's better, Dad. They're not discharging her, though. They say they have to keep testing her blood until the Bilirubin levels go down."

Doc Levy began rattling off numbers but Jack just tuned him out. He was wondering why Katie had said "better" instead of coming right out and assuring him that the baby was okay. But then he decided that it must be, because Richard was wheeling him into the nursery.

Doc Levy's beeper went off and Jack was the only one who turned around to watch him go. He pulled at his daughter's hand. "Well, should we grab the kid and run?" he asked her.

"What?" he heard Richard ask sharply, but Katie sighed and said, "Oh, Daddy, you don't know how bad I want to." Then he was surprised—and even Richard looked surprised—to hear her laughing, "Oh, God—I knew you'd understand."

The room was full of tiny sleeping infants, swaddled in pink or blue blankets. Richard parked Jack's wheelchair before a bassinet whose card read: Baby Crawford. But before he would peek inside he tugged at Katie's hand again. He wanted to tell her that he loved her. He'd thought up the words on the ambulance ride, had carefully prepared a long speech. But when Katie leaned down to him what he said instead was, "I'm sorry."

"No, don't be sorry," Kate whispered in his ear. "I love you, Daddy." Jack nodded, glad that she was braver than him.

"Kate," Richard said, interrupting them, "I can't—you're not hatching any plots with your dad. Kate?"

Kate straightened her back and looked at her husband. "It's not a plot, honey—but I do have a plan. Why don't you go try to find out what room Dad's supposed to be in while I introduce him to the baby?"

So it was Katie who leaned into the bassinet and lifted up Jack's grandchild. "Here, Dad," she said, "Here she is. Her name is Grace Elizabeth," and she looked at him expectantly.

At first all Jack could see was a furry crown of black hair. But his opinion softened as Katie formed a cradle of his arms and placed the baby against his chest. "Well, now," was all Jack could say. It weighed almost nothing—another little rabbit—but breathing, screwing up her face to cry.

FORTY-SIX

"*Esat-tsanh dah shi nané.* Listen to the story," I will say, and then I'll lean down and, sounding a lot like your father, I'll explain that that's how the Navajo begin their tales.

If you've asked me to tell you how your Grandpa Jack died, I will start with his pickup truck barreling across the mesa, with not just his hands but also his teeth and his innards clenched with fear because he's just been shown the face of his own death. He's choking on the fear; it coats his throat like dust. And he's also very angry because your grandfather has proven more than once that he is indestructible. And at least as strong as both of those feelings is regret, because he sees in death not just his own ending but also an end to his entire family and a whole way of life.

But then I'll have to add another story, a fairy tale recited into the deep-water blue of an infant's eyes, about a rabbit of a girl, taut as a coiled spring, with over-long ears and bright eyes. She is a tiny bunny on the inside; her fear stunts her growth, makes her speech and movements awkward, keeps her head down to the page. Unlike her father's, her fear is nameless. She makes a point of not looking into faces.

Maybe this time I should include the story of how you got your magic name, so I'll have to go all the way back to eastern Texas and your Great-Great-Grandfather Jack with his a herd of longhorn cattle. Or maybe this story's really about how you came to be, so I'll start with how I thought your daddy looked like a lean wolf at the Walgreens store.

All of the stories share these events: the two fears implode the old trailer, and I'll say that's what causes my labor to begin. The scene is vivid orange and black, and *Tio Abuelo* Fred always squirts at the fire with the garden hose.

Your grandfather and the black dog, Hud, are blasted onto the Navajo Nation, and your grandfather lands deep in the earth. In this place, called a *kiva*, there are exactly five rattlesnakes, and I will tell you how carefully your grandfather aims his pistol before he shoots. Even so—bang!—the first time he misses. Now he only has five bullets left. Thunk, thunk, thunk, thunk . . . thunk.

But the gun won't save your grandpa from the ghosts of the Anasazi, or from his thirst and a badly broken leg. Maybe this is where the girl with two names fits in, and I'll say she galloped off on Ol' Midnight to search for your grandfather under every rock and ledge from here to the rez, just as the Medicine Man had instructed her. But the rez is so dark at night, the horse beneath her blacker still, and blackest of all is the girl's own past. She fears its hot pursuit, so she'll want so bad to thunder right over the *kiva* and keep on going. She won't be able to help that feeling, that's what she's always done—she's always run away. But this time she hears your *Tio Abuelo* Fred calling—she *hears* him. And she comes back to help him, to be your sister.

So the black dog is forced to leave Jack and go for help, and finally, miles away, he catches the scent of mutton and follows it to the *hogan* of an old woman. She's afraid when she sees this black dog with a tongue that flops around his mouth like a thick, pink snake. The dog climbs inside her water trough and lies there, panting, lapping, slobbering, until she comes outside to chase it away.

I'll describe Hud rising out of the water and shaking, then trotting up to the woman to lie down at her feet. He's still panting but he stops to look back over his shoulder, and the way his lip catches on his big canine tooth makes the old woman wonder what he's trying to say.

You are being born, I will tell you, right as this is happening! And in my story, the timing is perfect; you come sliding out into the light just as your grandfather is lifted up to earth by the angels.

The way I will tell it, the black dog leads your grandfather straight to where we're waiting for him at the hospital, then Hud will snarl and bare his teeth at the guards who try to prevent Grandpa from holding you. After that, we don't let you go. For the next three days, you eat and sleep in my or your grandpa's arms. Somehow your birth turned that rabbit into a wolf, and the only other person who's ever allowed to touch you is your father while he changes your diapers.

Again and again over those three days, starchy, white beasts will prick your heel and snarl over your bright blood. But the lesson we are all learning is that some suffering is necessary; pains and disappointment—these, as much as our joys, make us who we are. So we submit to them as gracefully as we can, and for three nights I will snatch at sleep while your daddy wedges himself into the laps of two chairs and your grandpa snores. We're camped out in Grandpa's room, and I know the nurses think we're real hicks from the back country, especially after *Tio Abuelo* Fred, Chuck and Tom leave Rose to hold down the fort and come to visit us like the three wise men, their hats in their hands, shedding trail dust on the white vinyl tiles and reeking not of incense but manure.

Each night at 3 a.m. I'm jolted awake for another feeding, the joyously simple cure for the jaundice you were born with, and I'll tell you how I lunge for the phone and hear the nurse's voice, then your father speaking in the darkness, asking me if I want him to come with me. Then Grandpa rolls over and growls at Richard, telling him he ought to go home instead of sleeping curled in those chairs like a slug. Your daddy doesn't answer him, but calls, "Goodnight," to me as I'm leaving the room, and Grandpa answers, "Sleep tight," automatically, which makes your father snicker, so it's the sound of their laughter that follows me down the corridor.

In the elevator I hear other voices, women's voices. I hear my Great-Grandmother Grace's tough Irish and Grandma Elizabeth's complaining twang and my mother Lucy's city-girl wit. The doors slide open to the second floor and I slap down the hall in my slippers, answering yet another voice, the one that carries into the future: yours.

And, once again, I will lift you up, and I'll tell you again the same stories. I know it's never exactly the story that you've asked for. I guess I don't know the story about how your Grandpa Jack died, because always, in this story, Grandpa Jack, his people, his dog, and even his cows, live.

To be continued in
Book Three of
The Arizona Series: *The Last Creation*

Acknowledgements:

Many thanks to Judith Van, Dan Breazeale, and my husband, Dean Stover, for their invaluable assistance in the creation of this manuscript.

Book Cover Art by SelfPubBookCovers.com/Island.

J-Bar brand design by Deanna Stover.

Navajo creation stories were derived from Paul G. Zolbrod's *Diné Bahané: The Navajo Creation Story*. Albuquerque: U of New Mexico P, 1984.

About the Author:

Jan Kelly is a native Arizonan with an MFA in Creative Writing from Arizona State University where she taught for thirty years. She has one daughter and lives with her husband in Scottsdale, Arizona.

Don't miss out!

Visit the website below and you can sign up to receive emails whenever Jan Kelly publishes a new book. There's no charge and no obligation.

https://books2read.com/r/B-A-GZKDB-YUPVC

Also by Jan Kelly

The Arizona Series
Elder Brother's Maze
Jack Rabbit
The Last Creation
Sacred Arrow
People of the Sun

Watch for more at https://ReadJanKelly.com.

About the Author

Jan Kelly is a native Arizonan with an MFA in Creative Writing from Arizona State University where she taught for thirty years. She has one daughter and lives with her husband in Scottsdale, Arizona.

She is the author of The Arizona Series, novels intertwining Native American mythologies with western/adventure/romances set in the modern American West.

Read more at https://ReadJanKelly.com.